"We aren't finished, Nadine! Not until I say so!"

"You did say so," she bitterly reminded him. "We got divorced, remember!"

"Words," he bit out. "Just words on paper, a lot of legal babble. Whatever the law says, the truth is we're still connected, Nadine. There's a chain binding us and it hasn't broken." He put his hand on her thigh and she jumped, stiffening tensely.

"Don't."

"Yes. You can feel it. I feel it. Whether I'm touching you or not, whether I'm even with you or not, we're still connected, still linked." His voice dropped, deepened, murmuring huskily. "We're one flesh, Nadine. I'm only just beginning to understand what that means...."

CHARLOTTE LAMB is one of Harlequin's best-loved and bestselling authors. Her extraordinary career has helped shape the face of romance fiction around the world.

Born in the East End of London, Charlotte spent her early childhood moving from relative to relative to escape the bombings of World War II. After working as a secretary in the BBC's European department, she married a political reporter who wrote for the *Times*. Charlotte recalls that it was at his suggestion that she began to write, "because it was one job I could do without having to leave our children." Charlotte and her family now live on the Isle of Man.

Books by Charlotte Lamb

HARLEQUIN PRESENTS PLUS

1560—SLEEPING PARTNERS
1584—FORBIDDEN FRUIT

HARLEQUIN PRESENTS

1480—SHOTGUN WEDDING
1618—DREAMING

BARBARY WHARF

1498—BESIEGED
1509—BATTLE FOR POSSESSION
1513—TOO CLOSE FOR COMFORT
1522—PLAYING HARD TO GET
1530—A SWEET ADDICTION
1540—SURRENDER

CHARLOTTE LAMB

Fire in the Blood

Harlequin Books

TORONTO • NEW YORK • LONDON
AMSTERDAM • PARIS • SYDNEY • HAMBURG
STOCKHOLM • ATHENS • TOKYO • MILAN
MADRID • WARSAW • BUDAPEST • AUCKLAND

ISBN 0-373-11658-6

FIRE IN THE BLOOD

This edition published by arrangement with Harlequin Enterprises B. V.

Printed in U.S.A.

CHAPTER ONE

THE first day of April in London, April Fool's day in England, April Fish day in France, and nature was playing a typical April trick on the city, beginning the day with bright sunshine which deceived Londoners into going to work without a raincoat, only to send dark clouds scudding across the sky at around ten o'clock, followed up with a sudden thunderstorm at about eleven which had people running through the streets, sheltering in doorways.

It was still pouring with rain when the taxi dropped Nadine off outside the television centre just before midday. She opened her little yellow silk umbrella before she got out of the taxi, then ran inside, so that the wind howling across the car park shouldn't wreck her chestnut hair, which had just been expensively restyled at the hairdresser's. Usually any men she passed would stop and stare, amazed to see such a famous face passing by, but today the weather made her practically invisible. Everyone was too busy trying not to get too wet to have time to look at her. Even the taxi driver had failed to recognise her, although on the seat beside him lay a magazine whose cover carried a glossy photo of her in the latest look from Paris.

The electronic doors swished open automatically as she approached; she hurried through without lowering her umbrella, and collided with someone.

'Sorry!' she began, smiling, then looked up and froze on the spot, her hazel eyes widening and darkening in shock.

'Well, well, if it isn't Nadine!' he drawled, and the sound of his deep, smoky voice sent ice trickling down her spine.

She had not seen him for over a year, and had begun to think she was over the worst, but at that instant she realised she had been wrong, dead wrong. The worst had only just happened. She felt her body go into flight mode: heart racing, nerves tense, adrenalin going ready to flee.

She couldn't run, though. She had to play it quite a different way, look cool and unflustered, although she wasn't sure her voice was going to come out steadily. But she managed it.

'Good heavens, if it isn't Sean,' she said, taking time to shake her umbrella slightly to one side so as not to splash either of them before carefully closing it. It gave her an excuse for not meeting his eyes. 'What on earth are you doing here?' she asked lightly, finally looking up again. 'Don't tell me you've gone into television!'

He shrugged those wide, smoothly clothed shoulders while she watched and tried not to notice too much about him. Didn't she know exactly how he looked? He hadn't changed. But he was eye-riveting, and she couldn't help staring, although she told herself she was admiring the wide-lapelled black jacket, tight-fitting black jeans, black shirt, a scarlet silk tie the one splash of colour. Not many men would risk an outfit like that: meant to look casual, but with the stamp of a top French designer's flair. Jean-Paul Gaultier, she thought, his style perfect for Sean Carmichael's powerful build, the force of his body.

'I've just been on the Harper show.' His wide mouth twisted impatiently. 'The woman is some sort of idiot; she asked me all the same old questions I've been asked a hundred times, and didn't really listen to the answers. God knows why her ratings are so high.'

'People like her, she has a lot of charm,' Nadine said absently, trying to sound as calm as he did.

A year ago they had been hurling words like weapons at each other; it had been a bitterly fought divorce and she had thought she would never get over the pain of it, yet here they were just twelve months later talking politely, like the merest acquaintances. On the surface, at least. Underneath there was something very different, on her side, at least; but she wouldn't let herself think about that.

She thought about Juno Harper instead: a comfortably rounded woman, with softly silvering blonde hair and a warm smile, she had in her youth been a musical comedy star, and her new career as a chat-show host in her still glamorous fifties had brought out millions of loyal fans from her past to boost her viewing figures. She was popular with her famous guests, too, because she never asked awkward or embarrassing questions, was never malicious, never laid traps for unwary tongues, had a famous giggle for every comedian's jokes, was happy to puff a new film or book, and was invariably likeable.

'Her charm didn't work for me; she's too lightweight,' Sean said curtly. 'What about you? Are you here to do a programme?'

'No,' she said reluctantly. 'I'm here to see one of the producers; I'm auditioning for a new show.'

His eyebrows shot up. 'Acting? So you still have ambitions in that direction?'

'No,' she said sharply, a flush invading her creamy skin. She knew that tone—it was only too familiar, the sound of Sean in his sardonic vein. She had made several attempts to become an actress and failed dismally; had finally been forced to admit that she simply could not act. It hadn't been an easy admission for her, especially as she and Sean were drifting apart at the time. She had bitterly accused him of wanting her to fail; he had denied it but she was still convinced he hadn't wanted her to be an actress, any more than he had wanted her to model.

'No?' he drawled. 'So what are you doing here?'

'I'm having an interview with Greg Erroll,' she said shortly, but he still waited, his brows lifted and a quizzical expression on his face, so she felt compelled to expand her answer. 'He's looking for a female presenter for a new show he's going to launch in the autumn. It would be a morning show, an hour long; they want two presenters, a man and a woman.'

'Don't tell me . . . the man would do all the heavy stuff, the current affairs and serious interviews; and the woman would do the chatty interviews with other women, and the fashion and cookery and dieting!'

'Something like that,' she admitted, and Sean gave her a wry little smile.

'Well, never mind, if it is a huge success you could always use your muscle to get a better deal for yourself.'

She had to laugh at that. 'I haven't even got the job yet!'

'Always think ahead!' he said, as he had said to her so many times before, and she exchanged a grin with him, then could not believe this was happening. A year apart, and then within five minutes she felt as if they had never split up. It was a surreal experience; she could almost believe she was dreaming this encounter. She felt like pinching herself to make sure she was awake.

Instead she stared at him. At first she had thought he hadn't changed, but she saw suddenly how wrong she had been. Sean wasn't the same. He had always been slim, but she was sure he had lost some weight; he must have been working at full stretch over these months, and no doubt he had often forgotten to eat.

She remembered how he could forget everything but work, too obsessed to think of such mundane things as food, let alone her or any arrangement he might have made to meet her. Time had hardened his face: there was no spare flesh over that tough bone-structure, and there were some lines around his mouth and eyes that had not been there before.

He was still a magnetically attractive man, though: tall, slim-hipped, long-legged, dark, with brooding dark blue eyes and a strong, passionate mouth.

Their eyes met and held, and she felt a stab of such pain that she almost cried out with it.

Huskily, she said, 'I'd better go, I don't want to be late . . . goodbye, Sean . . .'

She didn't wait to hear his reply, she just fled, across the marble-floored foyer, towards the reception desk, where she muttered her name and was told to wait until Mr Erroll's assistant came down to escort her to the studio where they would be filming.

She had been nervous about the audition for a week, and meeting Sean on the way in hadn't helped, but Greg Erroll did his best to put her at her ease. He was one of the top men in television: an elegant, slightly built man in his early forties, who dressed formally in a dark grey suit and a crisp striped red and white shirt. He had a bland face which was deceptive; it was his piercingly intelligent grey eyes that warned you about the real man behind the calm façade.

Nadine was so tense that she blurted out, 'I've never been able to act, I'm afraid!' and Greg Erroll smiled soothingly at her.

'We don't want you to act, Nadine. We want you to be yourself, which is much harder than it sounds. Some people stiffen up in front of a camera, but I don't think you're going to do that because you're used to cameras, you feel at home with them, don't you?'

'After seven years of modelling I ought to!' she said, relaxing a little, conscious of the fact that the two cameras in the studio were focused on her at that moment, for she was able to see herself on the screen standing to one side. They had found her best side, the right one: she watched them exploring the height of her cheekbones, her faintly slanted hazel eyes, her wide, full mouth, closing in on her skin, showing every pore. Nadine watched with professional interest; her face was so familiar to her that she could view it quite impersonally as if it belonged to someone else.

'How does it feel to be so beautiful?' Greg Erroll asked, and she laughed, giving him a startled look.

'I'm not, though.' She was quite sincere in that, gesturing to her image on the screen. 'Look at my eyes—they're such a weird colour, nothing in particular, not green or brown or blue, a sort of mixture of all of them. I hate that, and I've always wished I had hair of a different colour; either black or blonde. My nose is much too thin, too long . . . and my mouth is much too big, it unbalances the rest of my face.'

He listened, smiling in his bland, dry fashion. 'So how do you explain your success as a model?'

'I've no idea, I've often wondered. Probably just luck. I started with such a brilliant photographer, Jamie Colbert—I owe my whole career to Jamie.' She broke off, looking around the studio at the clutter of electric cables, overhead tracking-lights, screens, cameras. 'Sorry, I'm talking too much; you want to start the audition, I expect.'

'We have started,' Greg said, looking amused. 'But now I want to swap chairs with you, Nadine.' He stood up, and she automatically did so too, a little puzzled. 'Sit here,' he said, and she obediently sat in his vacated chair. Greg looked up at a cameraman. 'OK for you, Rodney?'

'Could we move her a fraction to the right?'

Nadine began to shift her chair. Greg stopped her. 'Far enough.' He looked up at the cameraman again. 'How's that?'

'Back a bit,' Rodney said, and Nadine shifted again. 'Stop there!' Rodney told her. 'That's it. Perfect.'

They went through a similar check with the sound man, and the lighting man, who discovered a sheen on her forehead, a sudden outburst of perspiration, no doubt, due to nerves, which meant calling up the make-up girl to dab her temples with powder. At last, everyone was satisfied, and then Greg Erroll handed her a piece of paper.

'Now, Nadine, I want you to interview me. I've jotted down a few notes on myself; read it through and then we'll start.'

Nadine had known that she would be expected to do a dummy run of an interview, but she had imagined that she would be given far more time to read a profile of him, and think of some questions to ask, rehearse a little before they did it for real. Dry-mouthed, she looked down at the scribbled sheet and was relieved that she could at least read his writing. She read it through hurriedly, then again, more slowly, absorbing the information and surprised by some of it. She had had no idea, for instance, that Greg Erroll, had gone to a stage school as a boy, before going on to university; or that he had been married twice and had one child, a daughter.

'Ready?' Greg said, after the shortest five minutes in her life; and, taking a deep breath, Nadine nodded.

It was a baptism of fire, but because it was all so casual she found it easier than she had anticipated. She was nervous as she started, but once she and Greg were talking the questions came naturally because she was genuinely interested in him. He answered fluently most of the time, but once or twice clammed up, refusing to answer a question; and Nadine hurriedly went on to another topic, refusing to be thrown by the sudden blockage.

Greg suddenly called a halt, smiling as he got up. 'OK, that's it. Thanks, Nadine. I usually hate being interviewed, but with you it was fun.'

She stood up, too, a little shaky now that it was all over. 'Have we finished?' She couldn't believe it; the time had gone so fast. Huskily, she asked, 'How did I do? Was it OK?'

'I can't tell you until I've seen the run-through,' Greg told her cheerfully. 'Come on, I'll walk you to Reception.'

She had a sinking feeling that she hadn't impressed him, was not going to get the job.

'I have a few other people to look at before I make a decision,' he told her gently. 'But I won't keep you waiting for too long, I promise.'

Who else was he seeing? she wondered, but couldn't ask, of course. So she smiled hard and nodded.

'I understand.'

'You're a pro!' he said, guiding her back along the maze of corridors to the lift, in which they met Juno Harper, who was wearing a tailored black suit in which she managed to look sensuously professional. She glanced at Greg and gave him a quick, warm smile.

'Hello, darling, isn't this weather ghastly?' Her eyes drifted to Nadine with faint interest, then she did a double-take as she recognised her.

'Oh, hello, Nadine Carmichael, isn't it?' She extended a languid hand, the nails perfectly manicured, the skin soft and white. 'I've always wanted to interview you. Your face is everywhere these days.' She pulled a glossy magazine out from under her arm, waved it at Nadine. 'On the cover of this, for a start! I loved the outfit. Lucky you, going to all those fashion shows in Paris; I bet it was wonderful.'

'Wonderful, and hectic,' Nadine said, smiling back and liking her. 'They're all crazy when it comes to showtime.'

'Aren't we all, darling?' Juno laughed, then said, 'I tell you an odd coincidence, I just had your ex on my show—Sean. And the phone calls we got! I thought I was shock-proof but we had to filter out a lot of the calls. He shows up in a lot of ladies' fantasies, and they were dying to tell him all about them.'

Nadine pretended to laugh. 'Oh, dear!'

Juno's shrewd smiling eyes were like searchlights on her face. 'If I had ever had him I'd never have let him go, but then you switched him for Jamie Colbert, didn't you, you lucky girl? Some people have all the luck!'

Nadine's teeth hurt from smiling. She was very glad when the lift stopped and they all got out. She couldn't wait to get away; it had been a nerve-racking morning. She was glad it was over.

But it wasn't over yet. Juno had more to say, lingering in the marble-floored foyer and pretending to be unaware of the stares she got from a crowd of people queuing up to see an afternoon show which was televised live twice a week.

'So what are you doing chatting up our Greg? A little bird did whisper that you were in the running to be one of the presenters on the new morning show. Do I congratulate you or is it too early for that?'

'Don't be naughty, Juno,' Greg smoothly intervened. 'When we make the announcement you'll be the first to hear, don't worry.'

Juno gave him a sideways look, twinkling, unabashed, then said to Nadine, 'I should have had you on my show with Sean, you know. That would have made a very interesting programme. I didn't get much out of him; he's an oyster, isn't he? I couldn't get a syllable out of him about Fenella.'

Nadine's eyes didn't even flicker, although the name made her spine stiffen into rigidity.

Juno chatted on like a babbling brook. 'I asked him if they were getting married now they've finished filming this mini-series... what is it called? Why can I never remember film or book titles?'

'Because you aren't really interested in them, lovey,' said Greg, but obligingly supplied the title. '*Date with Death.*' He looked at Nadine's blank expression and thought she didn't know what he was talking about, so explained, 'It's that fat best-seller by the Frenchwoman, Anne-Marie Rossignol; some sort of psycho-babble about reincarnation and eternal love. It outsold everything else a couple of years ago. Remember it? Sean was clever enough to snap up the rights for a song before anyone else realised it was a hot property.'

'Not to mention lucky enough to have Fenella Nash just dying to make a film with him!' said Juno. 'And that gloomy-looking Frenchman playing the detective hero!'

'Yes, a good cast—it should be a big success for Sean,' Greg thought aloud, and Juno gave a thoughtful little frown.

'Should be, yes... but...'

Greg's stare went back to her sharply. 'You sound doubtful!'

Juno shrugged. 'I must admit I have a niggling little doubt or two—nothing definite, just a gut feeling. Sean didn't look like a man with a surefire hit in the can, and there have been whispers, you know how these things leak out even before the film gets to the cutting-room.'

Greg looked at Nadine, lifting his eyebrows. 'Have you heard anything?'

She shook her head. 'I don't move in the film world; how would I know what's going on?' But she couldn't help remembering the drawn look of Sean's face; the lines around eye and mouth, the grey tinge to the skin, that weariness she had never seen in his face before.

'Too bad for Sean if the series is a dud,' Juno murmured. 'He put up a lot of the money himself, which everybody knows is a crazy risk to take, but he had made a few million from *Dangerous Lady*, which was a huge hit, although personally I could never see why people made such a fuss about it, could you, Greg? Sean says he was only putting back into the company what he had made out of it so far, but that's just whistling in the dark. It was a mad gamble, and if his gamble doesn't come off it could be the end of Carmichael Films.'

'Don't be such a pessimist!' Greg said impatiently. 'I'd say that *Date with Death* has everything going for it—a great cast, a strong story, good writing, and a brilliant director. If Sean seemed down it was probably just exhaustion after months of filming. His adrenalin ran out, that's all. He'll be back on top by lunchtime tomorrow!' He looked at his watch, then kissed Nadine. 'I must run—be in touch soon, I promise.'

As he walked away Juno stared after him, her face thoughtful. 'Was I too pessimistic about Sean's mini-series? I didn't mean to be. It was just my instincts working overtime. I hope I'm wrong. Did you get the idea Greg had some sort of personal interest? I wonder if he's bought the series even before it has been edited? That would explain why he was so irritated by what I said. Oh, well, we'll soon find out if he has! Greg will have some difficult explaining to do to the board.' She gave Nadine a cheerfully naughty grin. 'Isn't life fun sometimes? I must go, too, darling. Can I give you a lift? My car's waiting outside.'

'No, thanks, my own car should be here soon,' Nadine said, and the other woman sauntered off, her rounded body swaying inside the sexily formal black suit. Even at her age men stared after her, and she enjoyed their attention.

As soon as Juno had vanished Nadine went out and hailed a taxi back to her Mayfair flat, feeling very bleak. Her mind was buzzing with everything Juno had told her. Sean was about to get married again. She had wondered when it would happen, but being prepared for it didn't make it any easier to accept.

He had been involved with Fenella Nash, the American actress who was starring in his latest production, ever since he and Nadine split up. She had frequently read rumours that they planned to marry, had thought that as soon as the divorce was through and he was free Sean would marry again, but it hadn't happened. Nadine had wondered if Fenella didn't want to tie herself down just yet. After all, she was one of the cinema's new sex symbols—a small, fiery redhead with bedroom eyes and a voice like whisky tumbling over ice. Even if she was in love with Sean her career would be the most important thing in her life.

Nadine didn't want to think about it any more. When she was back in her flat she stripped and took a shower, then went to lie on her bed, wearing just a terry-towelling bath-robe, witch-hazel-soaked pads on her eyes. Whenever she had had a bad day this was what she did to unwind: relax her body, empty her mind, so that the tension and stress seeped away.

Today, though, it didn't work. Her mind was jumping like a cat on hot tiles. Then the phone rang, making her jump. She sat up and took the pads off her eyes, lifted the receiver.

'Hello?' she said warily; she sometimes got very odd calls, even though she no longer had herself listed in the phone book.

'*Chérie*, you sound *distraite*!' a French voice murmured. 'Was it tough? It didn't go well?'

She relaxed, smiling. 'Oh, hello, Jamie. No, it wasn't difficult; in fact I enjoyed it, when I'd stopped being scared stiff! More than I thought I would. Greg got me to interview him on camera, and I found it really interesting; he's a fascinating man.'

'Terrific! So, it went well? You think you got the job?' Jamie Colbert's accent remained intensely French, despite the years he had spent in London, but he spoke English fluently, colloquially.

'God knows!' she groaned. 'Greg was very poker-faced, didn't give a thing away. I'll just have to wait and see.'

'I think you will get it,' Jamie said firmly. 'When they rang your agent first of all I was certain. They wanted you. Remember what she said...Greg Erroll had seen you being interviewed on television several times, and thought you would make a good chat-show host yourself. When they come looking for you, baby, they are really interested.'

'I hope you're right.'

'I always am,' he said with his usual dazzling self-confidence. Jamie was not a tall man, but he behaved as if he was—dominating the company in which he found himself, insisting on his own views, his own beliefs, aggressive towards other men at times, charming to women. He was a thin live-wire of a man of just over thirty, with black eyes and hair, a tanned olive skin, a face full of nervous energy and fire, and very, very French.

Nadine told him so, laughing. 'You're so French!'

'Chérie, tu es très gentille!' he said, gravely, then, dropping back into English, 'Nadine, you haven't forgotten we're having dinner tonight with the French ambassador?'

'Of course not! I'm really looking forward to it.' She was going as Jamie's guest, since Jamie was the guest of honour that night. One of France's most famous photographers, although he lived abroad, he had just won a highly coveted award with his latest book of photographs, which was to be presented to him tonight by the French ambassador, at a large dinner held in the French embassy in Knightsbridge.

'I thought you might be so excited after your audition that you had forgotten everything else!' Jamie said, a smile in his voice. 'OK, so I pick you up at seven. We have to be there at seven-thirty, for drinks before dinner at eight-fifteen. So be prompt, Nadine! We must not be late tonight.'

They weren't. They were early, and while they were waiting parked briefly outside a shop whose windows were full of televisions, all switched on, showing different channels.

'Oh, no! I don't believe it!' groaned Jamie and, startled, Nadine followed the direction of his gaze to find herself staring at Sean, his face filling a screen in a corner of the shop window. He was smiling faintly, but his eyes were shadowy and his facial muscles tight with tension.

Jamie said, 'What's the programme, I wonder? *Film Night?*'

Then the camera pulled back and Juno Harper came into view, laughing. 'It must be a repeat of the Juno Harper programme,' Nadine murmured. 'He was on it this morning; I bumped into him in the TV studios.'

Jamie shot her a look. 'I thought you looked rather harassed tonight. What happened?'

'Nothing—we were very polite to each other,' she said, then looked at her watch. 'Isn't it time we got going again? We don't want to be late.'

Jamie started the car again, his expression wry, but didn't say another word.

The ambassador already knew Jamie and greeted him like a friend before being introduced to Nadine and giving a Frenchman's approving glance at her figure. She was wearing a black silk and lace dress: a brief bodice which just cupped her breasts, leaving her white shoulders bare, tantalising with glimpses of the deep valley between her breasts; a stiffly layered skirt fell to her calf, flaring whenever she moved.

'St Laurent?' asked the ambassador's wife knowledgeably. 'Very chic.'

Tonight, though, Jamie was the centre of attention, the star of the evening; everyone wanted to talk to him, shake his hand, congratulate him, and Nadine left the limelight to him, rather relieved not to have to talk much, as they moved around the huge, chandelier-lit room. She smiled when introduced, replied if anyone spoke to her, but otherwise stayed in Jamie's shadow, finding it hard to follow the conversation because everyone spoke French, talking fast and furiously, their voices seeming to her English ear like the stuttering of machine-guns. Mostly she was silent, her mind elsewhere.

She was thinking about Sean, remembering the lines around eye and mouth, the weariness in his eyes, his pallor, wondering if Juno Harper had been right. Was his mini-series going to be a failure? But there were always disaster stories going around about projects like that; some people just loved to ill-wish anyone successful, and Sean's career had been one long success story.

On the way home, some hours later, Jamie gave her a frowning sideways look. 'You are very quiet, *chérie*. What is wrong?'

'Nothing,' she said, not willing to talk about what was on her mind. 'I'm just tired, I suppose.' A sigh wrenched her. 'This past month has been very hectic. I think I worked almost every day, except Sundays, and they were long days, some of them. I need a break, Jamie. I'm going to clear my diary and go away for a couple of weeks soon.'

She had been working hard for a year, in fact; ever since the divorce. It had been the only thing that saved her sanity; she had thrown herself into work to keep her mind busy and she had thought she had succeeded—she had been so sure that she was cured, that it was over. But seeing Sean again had thrown her back into the same old obsessed pattern; ever since this morning she had been thinking about nothing else, pretending to be speculating about his company, the mini-series, when she was constantly thinking about the way he looked: his brooding eyes, that sudden lop-sided smile which could charm or mock, the way his dark hair fell over his temples... Nadine broke off, biting her lip. There she went again.

Even when they were quarrelling bitterly, Sean had always been able to get a sensual response from her. Their chemistry, at least, had been a perfect match, but their marriage had been a battleground, and Nadine was terrified to find that she wasn't over him yet; he still had that effect on her, nerves like red-hot wires, pulses going crazy.

If she made a complete break, did nothing but lie on a beach and sunbathe for days, she might finally shut the door on the past and on Sean Carmichael.

'I wish I could come with you, but I'm too busy. Where will you go?' asked Jamie.

'Somewhere sunny and warm,' she said dreamily. 'The West Indies, the Canaries, Greece . . . I'll get some brochures tomorrow.'

It took longer to extricate herself from bookings than she had expected; her agent talked her into doing the next month's work but did manage to switch the jobs booked for the month after that to other girls, and meanwhile Nadine read brochures and daydreamed. She settled at last on a fortnight's holiday in the West Indies on a small island where she could not only enjoy lots of sunshine and clear blue seas but also learn to paint with a well-known artist whose wife ran the hotel. Nadine liked to sketch and painted water-colours in her spare time, although she had never had any formal training.

The day after she booked she heard from Greg Erroll. 'You've got the job,' he said cheerfully, and Nadine took a long breath, her face flushing and excitement making her stammer.

'Oh . . . oh, thank you! Oh, that's wonderful! I didn't really believe I'd get it, you know, thank you for letting me know so promptly and . . . Well . . . what happens now? I mean, when do I start work?'

He laughed. 'Not quite yet! We won't need you until the end of August; months away. I'll be in touch with your agent and arrange a contract; I'll discuss all the details with him so that he can re-arrange your diary and cancel any modelling jobs from September. But you had better be prepared to do publicity when we release the news; you're bound to be wanted for media interviews.'

'When will you release it?'

'Next week, I think, if your agent says you have time free for interviews. We want to get some good pre-publicity, we'll follow that up just before the show starts, but it is always useful to trail a new show months ahead.'

'I've just booked a holiday in the West Indies starting in a month's time—should I cancel?' Nadine reluctantly asked, hoping he would say no.

He did. 'Good heavens, no! The West Indies? Lucky girl, I wish I could get away but I'm too busy. No, go ahead, have your holiday. By then you should have done all the media interviews. They'll come in a rush, and any requests that come later can be put off until you return from holiday.'

He was right: when the announcement was made she did get an immediate rush of demands for interviews, but Nadine was used to talking to the Press and felt she did quite well, although some of the reporters asked what she considered to be outrageously personal questions.

One in particular, a columnist on one of the trashier papers, asked, 'Are you living with Jamie Colbert?'

'No, I am not!' said Nadine, bristling.

'But he is your lover?' the woman pressed, undeterred. Short and blonde, wearing a designer-label pink suit, she was very pretty, and as full of venom as a coiled cobra. Nadine had been warned about her by her agent in advance, and he hadn't been over-estimating her nastiness.

Coldly, Nadine said, 'Jamie Colbert has nothing to do with my new job! And I don't want to talk about my private life.'

Ignoring this declaration, the blonde purred, 'But you and he have been close for years, haven't you? You were still seeing him while you were married to Sean Carmichael. Wasn't he cited in the divorce?'

'No, he was not!' Nadine said through her teeth. 'If you had taken the trouble to check, you'd have discovered that our divorce was on the grounds of irretrievable breakdown of the marriage. Nobody else was involved.' She got up, looking at her watch. 'Now, if you'll excuse me, I have other appointments.'

'I haven't finished my interview yet!'

'You have,' Nadine said, on her way to the door of her flat to open it pointedly.

The columnist gave her a catty little smile. 'Well, if you don't really need the publicity, that's up to you...but I haven't really got anything worth printing here, and I think City TV isn't going to be too happy not to get a mention in my column.'

Nadine just held the door open and waited.

The blonde furiously collected her possessions and walked towards her, and as a parting shot said spitefully, 'Hoping there's a chance you might get back together with Sean now he and Fenella have split up, are you, darling?'

Nadine couldn't quite control her face and the reporter, fast as a snake, saw the way her skin tightened and paled, and smiled at having drawn blood.

'Oh, didn't you know? Yes, she flew back to the States this morning, and gave an interview at Heathrow saying it was all over between her and Sean. And the word is out that *Date with Death*, this TV mini-series they just made, is the worst disaster since the *Titanic*, and that's why she has dumped Sean. Not that she would answer any questions about that, and she denied that the series was a flop, but then she would, wouldn't she? She's an ambitious girlie, our Fenella, and if the series bombs out Sean Carmichael stands to lose everything, including his shirt, making him a less than desirable proposition for someone like Fenella.'

'Goodbye,' Nadine said, almost pushing the woman out of the door and slamming it.

For several minutes she stood there, leaning on the door, breathing thickly, her mind whirling. Only a couple of weeks ago Juno Harper had told her that Sean was going to marry Fenella, and now Fenella was on her way back to the States saying it was all over between them, there wasn't going to be any marriage. Was the blonde columnist's verdict the right one? Had Fenella dumped Sean because the mini-series they'd been making was a failure?

Next day she was able to read all about it in the popular Press, which went to town with photos of Fenella and Sean and interviews with Fenella. There was no quote from Sean. The papers all said that he was not giving interviews, and his staff answered telephone calls with one phrase: 'No comment.' That didn't stop the Press from speculating, naturally; the gossip columns were thick with innuendo, hints and half-truths.

Nadine wished she knew how Sean felt. Had he been in love with Fenella? That thought made her wince and hope he was miserable. He deserved it.

She only had a few more interviews to do during the fortnight that followed, and then she started packing to fly to the West Indies. She didn't need to buy any clothes: her wardrobe was full of sundresses, sandals, tops, shorts, beachwear which she had worn for photographic sessions but never on a beach yet.

She was leaving on a noonday plane, and when her doorbell rang sharply at nine o'clock she supposed it was the taxi she had booked, arriving earlier than planned to pick her up. She ran to answer it, intending to ask the driver to wait a few minutes, but the man on the doorstep was Larry Dean, one of Sean's closest colleagues in Carmichael Films.

'Larry!' Nadine was startled, her hazel eyes widening and darkening in shock. 'Hello. Good heavens. How are you? It's ages since I saw you.'

'I've got to talk to you, Nadine,' he said huskily. He was in charge of accounts in the film company; Sean had always said Larry was a genius with an account ledger. A big man physically, broad-shouldered, tall, Larry was a little clumsy. He lacked co-ordination, was always dropping things or knocking them over. He wasn't a good-looking man, or even a striking one: his hair was brown, his eyes were brown, his skin was freckled; he had a big grin and an appealing personality, like a shaggy dog who wanted to be friends with everyone it met but kept falling over them. Nadine had always been fond of him, but since he was Sean's oldest friend she had not set eyes on Larry since she and Sean parted.

'Well, come in,' she said, wondering what he had to talk to her about. 'I'm afraid I'm being collected in about half an hour; I'm off to the West Indies on holiday. But come in . . . can I get you a drink? Coffee or tea?' She played the polite hostess, and smiled, but her mind worked overtime on what he was doing here like this, out of the blue. Something to do with Sean, obviously. Had he sent Larry to see her? Her heart turned over.

Larry followed her into the flat. 'I don't want anything to drink, thanks. I won't keep you long, Nadine.' He looked down at her from his six-foot-four height, his face pale and drawn. She had never seen Larry look so sombre, and her heart missed a beat.

'What's wrong, Larry?' she asked huskily, and his brown eyes searched her face, their expression pleading.

'Nadine, do you know where he is? I must know, Nadine—I'm really worried about him. It isn't like Sean to disappear without a word.'

CHAPTER TWO

'SEAN?' Nadine repeated, wondering what on earth made him think he would find Sean with her.

'Yes, Sean,' Larry said impatiently. 'Have you seen him? Did he come here?'

She shook her head, blankly, and Larry gave a groan.

'Oh, God, why is he such a fool? I thought even he could see . . . well, if he isn't with you, where is he? He wouldn't do anything crazy, would he?'

'What are you talking about? What is all this?' Nadine burst out, and Larry looked at her helplessly, his big hands hanging clenched at his sides, as dumb as an ox.

She took him by the arms and shook him, her slight strength making almost no impression on that solid bulk. 'What is it? Tell me, Larry, damn you! What's going on?'

His brown eyes suddenly held hostility, shocking her even more because she had never seen such a look in Larry's cheerful, friendly face before.

'It's all your fault!' he threw at her in a choked voice. 'You and that damned divorce settlement! You ruined him!'

Nadine froze. 'That isn't fair!' she stammered. She had been taken aback by the size of the settlement, it was true, but her lawyers had insisted that it was only fair taking into account Sean's enormous assets. They had seen balance sheets drawn up by Larry which showed the company to be worth in the region of a hundred million pounds, and had excitedly told her that they were sure they could get her a very large settlement.

Nadine had wearily told them not to bother, she didn't need the money, and, anyway, in the first year of her marriage she had invested in the film company a considerable part of the very large income she made from modelling. At the time Sean had been desperately looking for capital, and she had just signed up with a cosmetics firm to front a big media campaign. It had seemed providential to them both.

She had lent him most of her huge advance from the cosmetics firm without hesitating, and Sean had made over to her some shares in the company, although she had forgotten all about that until they split up.

Even during the divorce proceedings, in spite of the bitter wasteland which lay between her and Sean, she hadn't wanted his money; but her lawyers had taken a very different view.

They had worn her down with arguments, their faces incredulous at her folly. 'You helped him set the company up! You're entitled to a share in it now, even if your marriage is over!' they had insisted, and Nadine had been too miserable to go on arguing; she had let them go ahead with the claim they'd wanted to make against Sean. They had won. Sean hadn't really even contested it, she remembered; indeed, he had agreed that she had been a great help to him during the early years of his company, and the divorce court had ordered him to make over to her another block of shares, or the equivalent sum in money.

'He had to buy your shares back, remember?' Larry muttered, glowering at her. 'And he borrowed from the bank to do it and has had to pay a horrific amount of interest ever since.'

'I didn't ask him to buy the shares!' she protested, flushing angrily. 'He insisted!'

'What choice did he have? You might have sold them without telling him, and he couldn't risk having some outsider buy ten per cent of the shareholding. He could have found himself being forced out of control.'

'I wouldn't have done that!'

'He couldn't be certain you wouldn't, and while they were in your hands they were a permanent threat; he had to get them back, and it was borrowing that money that started all his troubles. While he owed the bank a million he couldn't persuade them to lend him any money when he ran into difficulties over the mini-series. He had to borrow elsewhere, at a much higher interest, and money started bleeding out of us. If the series had been a success we could have weathered the problem, recouped our money from sales. But...' Larry broke off, groaning. 'I shouldn't be talking about all this; Sean would kill me if he knew.'

Nadine was sure he was right about that. If Sean was in financial difficulty he wouldn't want anyone knowing about it. But something else was on her mind, and she had to know the answer to a question burning in her brain.

'Why did you think he might be here?' Why should Larry think Sean would come to her when he was in trouble? Her heart beat thick and fast and she was breathless as she watched Larry's frowning face and waited for him to answer.

'I told him to come,' Larry muttered reluctantly, and her hazel eyes opened wide in bewilderment.

'But... why...?'

Furiously Larry broke out, 'I said he was a fool not to ask you to hand that money back. On paper he may be worth a hundred million, but that's all it is—numbers on paper. He couldn't raise a hundred million, or a fraction of that, even if he sold the whole damn company! But he paid you in real money. Cash. It was a stupid gesture, and he's paying for it. So I told him to ask you to let him have it back, even if it was only as a loan until he could get out of this!'

'Oh,' Nadine said. 'Oh, I see. Well, he didn't—come here. Ask me.' The words came out disjointedly, her mouth stiff and cold.

She might have known. Had she really been stupid enough to hope that Sean might come to her when he was in trouble, that he might need her? Had she forgotten that Sean Carmichael didn't need anybody, never admitted a weakness, never apologised, never forgave?

Larry shot her an eager look. 'Would you? If he asked?'

Nadine coldly said, 'If he did, I'd discuss it with him,' and Larry, snubbed, flushed and gave her an even more hostile look.

'I see. Maybe Sean was right not to come. I couldn't believe you'd be that vindictive, but Sean has always been smarter at reading people than I am.'

Nadine stiffened at the insult, hardly believed Larry had said such a thing, it was so out of character.

Red-faced, he turned on his heel, almost knocking her over, and she followed him to the front door, biting her lip.

She was angry with him for talking to her like that, but her curiosity was stronger than her anger.

'What did you mean, you were afraid he might do something crazy?' she asked as Larry opened the door.

He stopped, turned, staring at her with an angry frown as if trying to decide whether or not to answer, but at last he did, hurling the words at her as if he wished they were rocks and could hurt her.

'Sean has to pay a very large sum to the bank before the end of the month. If he doesn't, we're in real trouble; the company may fold. Sean's so worried, I'm afraid he may...' He broke off, sighing heavily. 'Oh, I don't know, don't take any notice of me, I don't know what I'm saying any more.'

Nadine looked at him fixedly and was sure he did know. Larry wasn't the type to talk wildly; if he did so now it was because he had some serious cause for worry. From what he said, Sean must be desperate, and her chest constricted at the thought of Sean in that state of mind.

Larry bleakly said, 'He could have paid the bank this month, but only if he didn't pay the salaries, so he paid the staff and it may be their last pay-packet, which some of them probably guess. Another of Sean's typically quixotic gestures. Sometimes I could hit him. If he would only think with his head, not his heart, we'd be much better off!'

'But you wouldn't like him so much!' Nadine said drily, and Larry gave a rough bark of laughter.

'No. Probably not.'

She thought soberly, frowning. 'What about the mini-series? That's finished; can't you raise money with it?'

Larry grimaced. 'Greg Erroll has pulled out of the deal we had set up with him. He had an option to take the mini-series but all this bad publicity about it has made him change his mind. So we won't be getting the fresh injection of money Sean thought we'd be getting from him, and that's what he was relying on to pay the bank.'

Nadine drew a shaken breath. So she had been right! Greg had intended to buy the series. But he had pulled out, presumably after hearing what Juno Harper had to say. That woman! Nadine thought bleakly.

Larry said flatly, 'We've both been everywhere we can think of, trying to find the money we need, but all we got were polite smiles. The word's out that the series is a mess and Sean's in trouble, and all the hyenas are out for his blood.'

'It's that serious?' she whispered, horrified.

Larry nodded grimly. 'Sean built that company up from nothing, and now some scavenger, some vulture, will come along and snatch it away from him, and all because of a couple of women! You and Fenella Nash! I could kill both of you! She started the landslide by talking to the Press and bad-mouthing the mini-series, and Sean has never been the same since you left, anyway.'

Her heart seemed to stop. He might just be talking wildly, but Larry had known Sean even longer than she had. She wanted to ask him what he meant, what made him think Sean had never been the same, but she couldn't. When he calmed down later Larry was going to regret half the things he had said to her today. It indicated how worried he was that he had been so indiscreet. Larry was a loyal, devoted friend: he kept saying that it was Sean who had built the company up but she knew that Larry had had a great deal to do with it too. It had been his financial expertise which had helped Sean get the company off the ground. In the beginning, when they were running Carmichael Films on a shoe-string, while Nadine was putting her modelling salary into the company to keep it afloat, and Sean was paying himself in peanuts, Larry had taken a tiny salary too, just enough to pay his rent and keep him fed.

By the time he'd married the company was doing better, but even so his wife, Virginia, who was an accountant too, with a financial institution in the City of London, had earned far more than Larry did, at first.

Just after Sean and Nadine split up, Virginia had stopped work to have her first baby, which was a little girl whom she had called Nadia. She had asked Nadine to be the baby's godmother, but although Nadine had wanted to accept she hadn't wanted to keep Sean away from the baby's christening party, and wasn't ready to face him again yet, so she had reluctantly backed out. Sean had been godfather, and no doubt he had been delighted to be asked. Sean loved children. He had badly wanted some of his own.

'And now he's disappeared,' Larry muttered then, and Nadine looked sharply at him, her skin icy cold.

'Disappeared?'

Larry nodded, his face tense. 'I haven't seen him for two days. I can't find him, and I've looked everywhere, believe me. It isn't like Sean to go off suddenly without leaving word where he was going. You know that. But that's what he's done. He just walked out of the office on Wednesday at lunchtime, and nobody has seen him since.'

Her lips white, Nadine said, 'He could have gone to the States, to see Fenella.'

Larry shook his head, looking irritable. 'Naturally I thought of that! I rang her; she hadn't seen him or heard from him. I didn't really think he would go to her; it's over between them.'

'It didn't last long, did it?' Nadine bitterly said. 'He left me for her just eighteen months ago, and now it's all over.'

Larry looked taken aback. 'Left you for her? Sean didn't leave you for Fenella Nash. You left him for Jamie Colbert!'

Nadine was furious; she gave Larry a bitter, antagonistic stare. 'You know better than that, Larry! You've always known what Sean was doing! He doesn't keep secrets from you!'

He didn't deny it, but protested, 'He told me your marriage broke up over Jamie Colbert!'

'Well, he lied. It isn't true. Sean walked out on me! He was making that first film with Fenella. *Dangerous Lady*. I never saw him, he was away on location for months, and when he did come home he was different, distant, not interested in me, I barely got a word out of him for weeks on end. Then the gossip about him and Fenella started; there were a few odd hints in gossip columns at first and then open comments, and when I faced him with it, asked him outright if he was having an affair with her, he didn't deny it.'

Larry was frowning, his face uncertain. 'And you weren't having an affair with Jamie Colbert before that?'

'No, I wasn't! Jamie was just the excuse Sean thought up for his affair with Fenella!'

'But I could have sworn——' Larry broke off as her doorbell rang loudly.

'My taxi.' Nadine bit her lip, her mind in chaos. 'I'm off to the West Indies today, on holiday,' she told him again.

The doorbell rang again and she groaned, hurrying to open the door. The driver gave her a grin. 'Sorry if I'm a bit late—traffic was terrible. You ready, miss?' He looked past her at the cases standing in the corridor. 'Can I take your luggage down for you?'

She nodded distractedly. 'Thanks. I... I won't be a minute...'

'Just want to check everything's turned off and nailed down?' he said cheerfully, picking up her cases. 'Don't take too long—will you?—or you'll miss your plane, and you don't want to do that.'

As he left, Nadine turned back to Larry, her face confused. 'Larry, have you tried his mother in the States?'

Larry grimaced. 'Well, I did, although I was sure Sean wouldn't have gone to her, as they've never been very close. She said she hadn't seen him for years.'

'No, we never saw much of her,' Nadine agreed, sighing. She had no family of her own, as both her parents were dead, and she had hoped to make friends with her mother-in-law, but Sean's mother lived in the States and was too busy to have time for her son. Sean's father had been dead for years and Sean had no other close family.

Nadine gave Larry an uncertain look. 'Sean isn't the type to lose his head. I expect he's gone off to see someone he hopes will lend him the money and was in such a hurry that he forgot to let anyone know where he was.' She looked round, picked up a glossy brochure from a table. 'Look, this is where I'll be. Ring me if you get any news.' She gave Larry a pleading look. 'You won't forget, will you?'

He shook his head. He looked so dispirited, so pale, that Nadine impulsively gave him a hug.

'Don't look so gloomy, Larry. Sean will think of something; he always does, doesn't he?'

His face lifted a little and he gave a faint smile. 'He always has, in the past,' he agreed.

'He will this time!' She heard the taxi hooting outside and sighed. 'I really must go, I'm sorry, Larry.' Quickly, she checked that she had everything she needed, and then Larry walked her out to the waiting taxi.

'Thought you'd changed your mind!' the driver grumbled, and, although it was a joke he was closer than he knew, because she was in two minds whether to go or not, but what could she do if she stayed? No doubt Sean would reappear some time today, but she wouldn't get her holiday, and she wouldn't get back the money she had already paid the travel agent.

'Sorry,' she said, then turned to hug Larry again. 'Have faith in Sean,' she whispered, and Larry kissed her.

'I will. You're right, I'm panicking too soon. Sean could be solving all our problems. Have a good holiday, Nadine.'

She waved as the taxi drove off, and thought he looked slightly less depressed than he had when he first arrived. She had cheered him up a little, but he had disturbed her. It had been easy to hate Sean when she'd thought he was making millions and riding the whirlwind of success. Now her emotions were in turmoil: she was anxious for him, concerned about the company, and guilty because her divorce settlement had put a strain on his finances. If she had known the true state of affairs she would never have let her lawyers ask for such a big settlement; she would have refused to sell her shares to Sean when he asked her. But he had never let a hint drop that he might be having money troubles; there had been no suspicion in her mind at all.

While she waited for her plane she swung in mood like a weather-vane: one minute deciding not to go, terrified that something might, after all, have happened to Sean, admitting that she wanted to be here, in case he needed her—and the next impatiently telling herself that nothing would have happened to him, Larry had been over-reacting, Sean was probably engrossed in fixing up a new deal to get himself through his current troubles, and if he had ever needed her he had a funny way of showing it.

Her flight was called and she sat there, staring at nothing, still undecided.

Oh, this was stupid! she thought, getting up, then stood there, dithering for a moment, before she finally made up her mind.

The journey was long and tiring, and before she finally reached her destination she had changed her mind back and forth a hundred times. By the time she was checking into her hotel she was in no state to think of anything other than that she was deeply relieved to have at last stopped travelling. She signed the register and stumbled along a corridor behind the porter carrying her bags. It was still daylight here; she had been reminded to turn back her watch just before her plane landed but in her head she was still in another time-zone. It felt like the middle of the night, but the sun still shone. Nadine was too disorientated to take in much about her surroundings, but she did realise that the single-storey hotel was larger than she had expected.

Her room was simply but elegantly furnished, that much she took in at a glance while she was tipping the porter. When he had gone, Nadine left her cases undisturbed but unpacked her small overnight bag, which held night things. Within ten minutes she was in bed, the shutters closed, the room dark, and she fell asleep immediately.

When she woke up she had a headache that was like being assaulted by pneumatic drills. Fumbling for the bedside lamp switch, she sat up, wincing with pain. She felt terrible. Jet-lag? she wondered as she groped for her watch and looked at the time. Four o'clock? Confused, she couldn't work out whether it was morning or afternoon, then realised it was four in the morning, and she had slept for eight hours.

Nadine groaned. Four in the morning. Everyone else would be asleep. She might as well try to go back to sleep herself. But first she needed to go to the bathroom. She slid out of bed, realised she was sweating, her body not yet accustomed to the different temperature here.

Her *en-suite* bathroom was all blue and white: the marble floor blue, bright Caribbean blue, with an inset mosaic in front of the bath, a large white dolphin splashing its tail in the blue sea. She was tempted to have a shower, but decided to take some aspirin first and try to get back to sleep.

She lay between sleep and waking for an hour or so, fretting over Sean, then put on the light again and looked around the room, yawning. Her headache had more or less gone, but she still felt distinctly jet-lagged.

She liked the décor of her room: it probably looked even better in sunlight. The marble floors were white, the modern furniture white with gold trimming, a wall-to-wall fitted wardrobe with louvre doors giving plenty of space for her clothes. There were large white stoneware lamps around the room, which was dominated by a kingsize bed, and a vase of vividly coloured flowers she couldn't name stood on a chest of drawers.

It was half-past five now. She got out of bed and tiptoed around, unpacking her clothes and putting them away. When she had finished, she had a refreshing shower, and put on a white towelling robe before opening the shutters on the full-length sliding glass door which made up the wall facing the wardrobe.

A large private balcony ran outside: Nadine opened the door and wandered, barefoot, out into the most beautiful sunrise she had ever seen. It took her breath away. The tender blue sky was streaked with flame and gold, the air was cool, birds were calling in the hotel gardens, their wings flicking as they flew from tree to tree, landing on bougainvillaea bushes, snapping up insects on the vivid flowers. There were smooth green lawns stretching down to a silvery white beach. A sprinkler system was already in operation, spraying the turf with whirling jets of water. Through the trees she glimpsed tennis courts, the blue water of a large, tiled pool in which someone was already swimming.

A swim. That might help her feel more human, and then she could have breakfast.

Five minutes later, Nadine was on her way through the trees to the blue gleam of the pool. By the time she reached it, it was empty. She padded across the marble-tiled surround, dropped her robe on to a lounger, and paused on the edge to dive into the water, which was still a little chill after the night. She swam several lengths, quite fast, then climbed out and put on her robe. It was a good start to the day. She felt much better. In fact, she was starving, so she hurried back to her room, showered again to rinse the chlorine out of her hair, and dressed in a simple yellow sundress, put on white sandals and went in search of a dining-room. Tomorrow she would eat her breakfast on her balcony, she decided, while she watched that miracle of a sunrise again.

She was not the only guest in the large dining-room. A man sat with his back to her behind a potted palm. Nadine hesitated, wondering where to sit, and a waiter arrived, beaming.

'Good morning, ma'am, I am Jacob, your breakfast waiter. Are you alone for breakfast? Would you like a table by a window? Please, sit down, here is a menu. Coffee? Juice? Do you want a cooked breakfast or can I bring you a Continental basket and some fruit?'

He left her reading the large menu while he went to get her a pot of coffee. Nadine enjoyed reading the list of cooked food, but she finally chose a cold meal. The waiter brought her a basket of rolls and breads, and then a bowl full of a mixture of fresh local fruit, some familiar, some she had never seen before. The waiter told her their names. 'This here is naseberry,' he said, pointing to something that looked vaguely like a grey avocado, but had pink flesh. 'This is ackee . . .' he added, looking at a brilliant scarlet fruit. He broke one open and showed her large, shiny black seeds buried in creamy yellow flesh.

'It looks like scrambled egg!' said Nadine and the waiter nodded.

'It don't taste like it!' He sliced through a round fruit. 'This here is called a star apple.'

'Oh, I've eaten that before, sliced in fruit salads, in England,' said Nadine. 'So that's what it is called—what a lovely name, star apple.'

'Very pretty name, ma'am,' the waiter agreed and left her to enjoy her breakfast while he went to serve some new arrivals, a family: husband, wife and two teenage children all with American accents.

Nadine was feeling much better as she left the dining-room. She looked at her watch and calculated the time in London. She wanted to ring Larry at the office and find out if Sean had shown up yet, but it would be lunchtime in London now, so she would wait a couple of hours.

She consulted the reception clerk about the art classes. 'Mr Haines always gives guests from England a day to recover from the journey before they start classes, madam. Your first class will be at nine o'clock tomorrow, but Mr Haines would like you to join him and your fellow students at a cocktail party this evening, before dinner.'

'Do we dress formally for that?'

'As you choose, madam; there are no rules here. You are on holiday, and we want you to relax and enjoy yourself.' He gave her a glossy brochure. 'All the details are in here.'

Nadine took the brochure back to her room and studied it sitting on her private balcony, watching the blue sky, the blue gleam of the pool, the vividly coloured birds among the lush green palms and bougainvillaea, while she waited to ring London.

She was put through to Larry at once: he sounded very far away and very tired. 'No, we haven't heard a word from him,' he said. 'But I was talking on the phone to an actor in Los Angeles who said he'd seen him there yesterday. I didn't want to start talk so I couldn't be too probing, but I got enough out of the guy to be sure he did see Sean there. So I've got my secretary ringing every good hotel to ask if he's staying there. If he is in LA we'll find him, and when I do I'll kill him for doing this to me!'

'Kill him for me, too,' Nadine said, almost light-headed with relief for an instant, and then furious with Sean. Typical of him to be so thoughtless, never thinking what his silence might be doing to people who cared about him. He should have known how Larry would worry.

When she had rung off she put on a vivid jade-green all-in-one swimsuit, and over that a filmy multi-coloured beach wrap, then collected a beach-towel, a novel she was reading, her headphones and some tapes, all of which she put into a large wicker basket, and made her way down to the hotel's private beach.

By now other guests were lying on loungers under gold and white striped umbrellas, but there was plenty of room and Nadine was soon stretched out, her skin oiled and glistening, to make sure she didn't overdo the sunbathing, eyes closed, her headphones over her ears, listening to the latest tape of one of her favourite groups. When she was bored with the music she switched it off and listened to the sound of the surf rolling up on the silvery beach, the whisper of the palms, while the sun poured down and made her feel immensely sleepy, in spite of the hours she had slept last night.

That evening she went down to the cocktail party given by Luc Haines, for the members of his art class. There were around a dozen people there; more women than men, noticed Nadine as she hovered by the door.

One of the five men in the room came across to meet her, holding out his hand. 'Hello, I'm Luc Haines.'

'Nadine Carmichael,' she said, shaking hands.

'Nadine,' he repeated. 'A beautiful name for a beautiful woman. I'd very much like to paint you, but we'll discuss that later!'

Nadine laughed a little uncertainly—had he recognised her? She couldn't tell from his face. He was a short, broad man with Mediterranean colouring, who looked much younger than she had expected, as she confessed to him.

'But there's a big photo of me in the brochure,' he pointed out, and Nadine hesitated.

'Yes, but... well, I suspected it might be a very old one, they often are, and you're so well known I thought you must have been working for years, and be much older than you looked in that photo,' she blurted out, flushing as he laughed out loud.

'I can see you are a very cynical lady. Remind me, have you had any art training?'

'No, I'm just an interested amateur. I sketch and paint water-colours occasionally. I enjoy it but I know I'm not very good. It's just a hobby.'

'If you enjoy it, that's all that matters. And I'll be the judge of whether or not you're any good. What do you do for a living, Nadine?' He had already announced that first names were always used in his class and she was finding it easy to call him Luc because he was so direct and friendly.

'Well...' She hesitated, frowning. She wasn't surprised or offended because her name obviously meant nothing to him. It was a relief, in fact. It was only in Britain and the States that people saw her on TV in the commercials she had done. Nadine preferred to be anonymous; it meant she met people without them having preconceived ideas about her.

Famous models seemed to have a certain reputation: jet-setting, nightclubbing, hobnobbing with pop stars. That was what people expected if they knew you were a model. Nadine was tempted not to tell Luc Haines the truth, but what if another guest recognised her?

Luc was watching her expectantly, his face curious. 'You prefer not to say? I wonder—is it something exciting, or tedious? Well, never mind, forget I asked. Come and meet your fellow students.'

Nadine was nervous at first, afraid as she shook hands with them one by one, that somebody was going to say, 'But aren't you Nadine Carmichael, the model in that TV ad?'

Nobody did, nor was she pressed to tell them what she did, because Luc said wickedly, 'Nadine prefers to forget real life while she's here, so we won't ask her personal questions, will we?' and everybody looked at Nadine with surprised amusement and laughed.

'Same for me!' several of them chimed, grinning at each other.

'Let's all forget our lives back home,' another younger woman said eagerly. 'Don't you wish you lived here all year round?' and the others all sighed, as if they certainly did. By the end of the evening they had already become a group and were chattering easily to each other as they left the hotel dining-room after an excellent meal.

Nadine went to bed early, still slightly suffering from jet-lag, but also because she wanted to be fresh and full of energy next day. She fell asleep at once and slept heavily.

Towards dawn she had an incredibly vivid dream. In it, she was not divorced from Sean; they were together, in bed, making love. Sean was kissing her throat, making her tremble as she felt the sensuous slide of his naked body against hers.

Nadine moaned, restlessly moving in the bed, beginning to wake up, and as she did so she realised suddenly, with a panic-stricken jolt that woke her up faster, that her dream had not been a dream. She was not alone in the bed. There was a naked body next to hers, a man's body; his mouth was on her throat and his hands were everywhere, caressing her breasts, stroking her softly, intimately, sliding down her thighs.

CHAPTER THREE

NADINE began to scream and at the same time sat up and began scrambling out of bed. The man beside her acted even faster. He grabbed her before she could get away: a hand clamped down over her mouth while he pulled her back down again into the bed, kicking and struggling. He rolled on top of her in spite of her efforts, holding her down with the sheer weight of his body.

Nadine was suffocating, and scared witless with panic: she gasped and choked, trying to see him, but was half blinded by her tangled chestnut hair which had fallen over her eyes.

Her senses told her too many things all at once: the muscled power imposing itself on her, the silken feel of his bare, tanned skin against her own, the salty taste of his palm over her mouth. Through her hair she was getting glimpses of wide, brown shoulders, a strong neck, black hair. A mouth.

She stiffened, lay still, staring up at that mouth: the hard, sardonic curve of the upper lip, the full, sexy promise of the lower one.

'Promise not to scream again,' the mouth said softly.

Nadine bit it.

The mouth swore. The hand was snatched away. 'That damned well hurt, you vicious little cat!'

'Good,' Nadine said, shifting her head on the pillow so that her hair fell back and she could see his face. She wished she could look at him with unmixed dislike, but for some stupid reason she felt an overwhelming relief that he seemed so fit and well. Why are you such a fool? she asked herself angrily, and told Sean aloud, 'Served you right, gagging me like that!'

'I had to, before you woke up the whole hotel!' Typically he was unrepentant, he looked at her as if she was the one being unreasonable, and her teeth met.

'I promise you this much,' she said through her clamped teeth. 'If you don't get off me, and out of my bed, I'll scream so loudly I won't just wake up the hotel, I'll wake up the whole island!'

'Vixen!' he said, but began to slide off her. He didn't exactly hurry, though; his naked body slowly rippled sideways. Like a snake, she thought bitterly. A long, silkily rippling snake uncoiling against her. He was prolonging the contact deliberately, tormenting her, and Nadine wanted to hit him because he knew what he was doing to her, just as she knew only too well that he was sexually aroused.

As soon as she was free to move she did, practically falling off the bed and grabbing up her silk robe from a chair beside the bed, hurriedly sliding her arms into it, aware all the time of Sean watching her from the bed although she had her back to him. Her hands trembled as she pulled the silk belt tight around her waist then she swung round to face him.

'Now, what the hell are you doing in my hotel room?'

'The hotel didn't have another room free,' Sean drawled, stretching lazily under the crumpled sheet. Nadine tried not to look but even half-covered his body was like a magnet to her eyes.

'Then go to another hotel!'

'There isn't one, apparently.' He gave her a bland smile. 'This is a very small island. So, as I was your husband, they gave me a key to your suite.'

'They had no right to do that!' she burst out, quivering with temper. 'Not without checking with me first!'

'It was after midnight, your room was dark, and we thought you might have jet-lag so we didn't want to wake you up,' he said smoothly.

Her hazel eyes glittered furiously. 'You mean *you* didn't! If they had woken me up I would have told them you aren't my husband any more!'

He ignored the interruption. 'I was able to show them my passport, to prove my identity, of course; but the clincher was when I showed them a snapshot of us on our wedding day, which I happened to have in my wallet.'

'Well, what a coincidence that you happened to have that with you!' Nadine snarled, and he gave her a reproving look.

'You're being very nasty. It must be because you were woken up so early. You see why I didn't want to wake you up last night when I arrived. You would probably have been even nastier. As I said to the reception clerk, I know what you're like if you're woken up when you need a good sleep.'

Nadine seethed. 'Oh, very clever! Well, it won't do you any good. I am not...repeat not...sharing a room with you!'

Sean yawned, deliberately, widely, and stretched again, his arms over his head and his powerful body outlined under the sheet in a way that made Nadine look away, swallowing convulsively.

She babbled to disguise her reaction. 'How you have the nerve to think I would baffles me! You can just get out of here now, and I don't care if there's no other room available. You can sleep on the beach or under a palm tree, or take the next plane back to London! One thing is certain: you are not sharing my room!'

Sean sat up and Nadine's eyes flickered, her face burning with colour as she looked at his broad, gleaming brown shoulders and the dark curling hair growing down to that taut, muscled midriff.

'And get your clothes on!' she muttered.

'OK,' he meekly agreed, and threw back the sheet. Nadine's mouth went dry as her senses registered the full impact of that lithe naked body. It was the first time she had seen him nude for years, and she was horrified to realise that the passage of time had done nothing to diminish his effect on her.

She turned her back again in a hurry and heard him laugh softly. That made her even more furious, then her nerves jumped as he came round the bed towards her.

'What are you doing?' She flung round again to confront him, her eyes wide and dilated as she saw him right next to her.

'Getting dressed,' he said, face innocent. 'I thought that was what you wanted me to do!' He gestured and Nadine looked round in confusion, and saw a pile of clothes on a chair, beside which stood a large suitcase.

'Oh.' Her flush deepened as she felt him silently laughing at her. 'Yes, well, get dressed, then,' she crossly muttered, and walked away, over to the window to open the shutters. Light streamed into the room, the sun was up and the sky already bright blue. Behind her she heard a click. Sean had opened his case. There was the sound of rummaging fingers, telling her he was looking for clean clothes to wear; then the rustle of material as he put something on.

'Can I take a shower?' he asked, and Nadine swung round to glare at him.

'No, you can't!' He hadn't put on clothes at all, she saw, infuriated. 'I haven't had my shower yet,' she told him, 'and anyway, I want you out of here now.'

'Don't be so selfish. I'll only be here one day—I'll be leaving tomorrow.'

'You can leave today.'

'No, I can't,' he said triumphantly. 'There's no boat on a Sunday; the next boat is tomorrow. That's why I arrived so late last night. I flew in on the only plane yesterday and had to spend ages haggling over the hire of a boat because I'd missed the daily run, and there wasn't one coming over here until Monday.'

'Well, the hotel will have to find you a bed somewhere else until then. When I've had my shower and dressed I'll explain to them that you are no longer my husband and you cannot share my room!'

'I did,' he said in those maddeningly reasonable tones. 'Last night.'

Nadine's heart skipped a beat. She suddenly remembered waking up from that dream of Sean making love to her. She stared at him fixedly, her face very hot, her eyes searching his face for clues. Exactly what had happened during the night? He had been in bed with her, naked, touching her...for how long? And was that all that had happened? Her dream came back to her in terrifying fragments. Sean kissing her. Sean's mouth on her nipples. Sean . . . Oh, God, she thought with a pang of rage and distress. Was I dreaming, or did it happen?

He smiled crookedly at her. 'Just like old times!' he drawled, and she lost her temper and flew at him, her hands curled into fists.

'You...you...' She tried to hit him but he caught her wrists and held her at arm's length, struggling and trying to kick him.

'Temper, temper!' It made her even angrier to see the amused satisfaction in his eyes.

'How dared you...how dared you...?' she hissed, trembling with fury.

'How dared I what?' he asked, pretending to be puzzled. 'Share your bed? What else could I do? I wasn't sleeping on that marble floor. It was a hot night but nobody could sleep on marble. And the chairs were impossible. I suppose I could have slept in the bath, but somehow that didn't occur to me.'

'Of course, it wouldn't!' she snapped.

He ignored that, calmly going on, 'Your bed was kingsize, there was plenty of room, and I was so shattered after travelling all day to get here that I fell asleep as soon as my head hit the pillow.'

She was tense, watching him like a mouse watching a cat outside its mousehole.

He watched her back, his hard mouth curling in that mocking smile she knew only too well. It warned her. Sean was enjoying himself. But she needed to know. Precisely what had happened last night in that bed?

'Until you woke me up,' he murmured. 'In that very interesting way!'

'What interesting way...?' she began, then swallowed and wished she hadn't asked, scalding colour rushing up her throat and face.

'Don't you remember?' He was having a lot of fun, tantalising her with hints, his eyes gleaming. 'Don't pretend you've forgotten, Nadine!'

Suddenly Nadine decided she didn't want to know after all. The way he was looking at her made the hairs stand up on the back of her neck.

'Oh, get dressed and get out of here!' she yelled at him, and Sean took the long stride needed to cover the space between them, his hand clamping down over her mouth again.

'Ssh,' he murmured. 'You don't want the manager coming up here because other guests have rung him to complain, do you?'

'Leggo!' she mumbled into his hand. She couldn't even bite him because he was being too clever: she couldn't get her teeth apart while his fingers gripped her cheekbones.

'What?'

'Let go!' she managed at last, and Sean took his hand away, too suddenly for her to have a chance to bite it.

She snapped at him instead. 'And get dressed!' Looking around desperately, she saw the open door of her bathroom and, hanging on it, a white towelling robe. She gestured. 'Put that on!'

Sean gave her a wry look, but obeyed without haste, strolling over to the door and taking down the robe, sliding his arms into it, tying the belt casually around his slim, firm waist before he turned back suddenly, catching her staring.

His eyes mocked her. 'Reminding yourself what you're missing, darling?'

Nadine had never been so angry. Well, not since the last time they'd had a monumental row, anyway. She could feel the blood rushing round her body, singing in her ears, making her pulses jump and leap.

'I'm going to complain to the manager about all this!' she promised hoarsely, snatching up the telephone from her bedside table.

'Of course, that's up to you,' drawled Sean, smiling that silky smile. 'But I wouldn't in your shoes.'

'Don't threaten me!'

'It's not a threat,' he said, opening his blue eyes and looking hurt. 'I was just trying to point out that you hadn't really thought this thing through.'

She waited, eyes needle-sharp, knowing that he was about to detonate some bomb right underneath her. She knew that expression on Sean's face and it always meant trouble for someone. Usually her.

'After all,' he said softly, 'If you tell the manager that we're divorced, and complain about having me in your bed last night, there is no chance...no chance whatever, I'd say...that you're going to keep that little item out of the gossip columns.'

She registered that, biting her lip. 'She wouldn't tell the Press!'

'She?' He looked surprised. 'The manager is a woman? I've never before stayed in a hotel which had a woman manager.'

'I think she and her husband own it. He's Luc Haines, the artist—I gave you one of his pictures once, remember? A water-colour of a fish market.'

'That one? I still have it,' said Sean. 'So he lives on this island and owns the hotel? What a coincidence.'

'It's nothing of the sort. That's why I'm here. He holds art courses based on this hotel; you spend half the day painting and the other half on the beach. I've always enjoyed painting water-colours, so I decided to take the course and have a holiday at the same time. Didn't Larry tell you that?'

'He said you seemed upset and tired and he thought you needed a holiday,' Sean admitted, and they were both silent for a long moment, looking at each other. Nadine searched his face and saw the deep lines she had seen before, the grey weariness under his usual tan. Sean needed a holiday, too; he looked as if he needed to sleep for a week. She wondered what he saw in her face—the same exhausted look she saw in his? She wouldn't be surprised. She had been under a strain ever since the divorce, emotionally, mentally, physically. She felt as if she had been running a very long race and she wanted to stop and lie down.

Quietly, Sean said, 'Anyway, last night when I checked in I only saw a male reception clerk, and he obviously didn't have an idea who I was! Or who you were, come to that. He wasn't just being discreet. He really didn't know who we were! You know how you can always tell when people have recognised you; there's that look in their eyes.'

'Yes,' she had to concede. You could always tell, even when they tried to hide it. There was that telltale flicker, the look of surprise, of recognition.

Sean shrugged. 'But if you make waves . . . complain . . . tell them we're divorced, but I spent the night with you . . .'

Her eyes flashed. 'Don't keep putting it like that! You may have spent the night in my suite, but not with me!'

'In your bed, then,' he mocked, and she gritted her teeth and glared at him.

'I won't tell them that!'

'Where will you say I slept, then?'

She was furiously silent, and he grinned at her wickedly. 'Whichever way you put it, if you make a fuss you're going to arouse a lot of curiosity. It's too good a story; they're going to talk about it, among themselves, and there must be a local newspaper. Someone on the staff is bound to sell the story to a reporter.'

Nadine frowned, pushing her heavy chestnut hair back from her flushed face. 'I don't believe it! It would be very bad publicity for the hotel, after all, letting you walk into my room in the middle of the night without checking with me first!'

'Maybe the management wouldn't sell the story, but the hotel staff would chatter about it among themselves and tell their friends, and sooner or later it would get to the ears of a reporter, and our names would ring a bell.'

'Especially yours!' she muttered, scowling.

'I have had a lot of Press coverage lately,' he drily agreed. 'The local reporter would sell the story to the American Press and the next thing you know we'll be up to our necks in reporters. Come on! Think about it! If you read that story in a gossip column, wouldn't you laugh like mad? Divorced wife wakes up to find her ex-husband in bed with her in hotel room?' Sean started to laugh.

Nadine didn't. She eyed him coldly. 'I don't think it's remotely funny!'

'Well, your sense of humour was always defective,' he murmured. 'But believe me, my darling, if you open this particular Pandora's box you're going to find yourself wishing you hadn't.'

He had convinced her, but that just made her angrier and she burst out, 'Just get dressed and get out of my suite! If they haven't got another room, hire a boat again and book into another hotel! I'm sure you'll come up with something.'

'Oh, stop shouting!' Sean snapped back at her, his brows heavy over his brooding blue eyes. 'I only had a few hours' sleep and I'm in no mood for all this aggro!' He walked towards the bathroom. 'I'm going to have a shower!'

'I want one!' she protested, but he was already inside the bathroom and closing the door.

'You'll have to wait, then!'

'You selfish . . .' she began, then stopped in frustration as she heard the shower start to run. He couldn't hear her so there was no point in telling him what she thought of him yet. She would save it up for later.

She went out on to her balcony and leaned on the balustrade, her mind working busily. Three guesses why Sean had followed her here! You didn't need to be a genius to work it out! As soon as Larry tracked him down and told him she was in the West Indies they had plotted together, worked out that while she was here, and, alone, she would be an easy target; and Sean had set off to join her.

No doubt he thought he had made a brilliant beginning. She brooded resentfully on that thought.

That snake had got back into her bed last night, and she still didn't know exactly what had happened.

Something had. That had been a very vivid dream and she had woken up to find it actually happening. How much else of that dream had actually happened?

She trembled, closing her eyes briefly. No! She didn't want to know that.

She thought about something less disturbing. Money. The reason for Sean's arrival here. Larry was determined to get her to hand back her divorce settlement or lend it to the company; and Sean, having obviously failed to raise money during his trip to Los Angeles to hunt for backing, had finally agreed to ask her for it.

She had to admit, it was a big point in his favour that Sean hadn't wanted to ask her, had tried every other avenue first. If she was to believe Larry, that was!

But he was here, now, wasn't he? she cynically thought. If he was so scrupulous and reluctant to ask her for the money, how come, now that he actually was here, he was ruthlessly prepared to use every weapon he could get his hands on?

It didn't add up, did it? Never mind what Larry said, she told herself. Look at what had actually happened. Last night, Sean had crept into her bed, made love to her, then blackmailed her to stop her complaining to the hotel management...

Nadine watched some children in the hotel pool, their laughter and the splash of their dives into the blue water quite clear and sharp in the morning stillness. The blue sea glittered with sunlight. Her mind glittered like broken glass, bright and sharp and dangerous.

She was looking ahead, guessing what was going to happen next. Sean was not going to obey her meekly, leave the island at once, give up his attempt to get his money back. This was only the start of his campaign.

But one thing she was determined about. He was not sharing this room!

She heard the bathroom door open and gave a quick look round to check that he wasn't naked before she walked across the bedroom to take her own shower.

Without looking at him she curtly said, 'When I come out I want to find you gone!'

She didn't wait for a reply, just collected a few clothes, went into the bathroom and bolted the door.

He had left the room untidy, as usual. She crossly picked up the damp bath-sheet he had flung over the side of the bath, shook it and hung it on the hot hotel rail to dry, smoothed out the bath-mat, put the cap back on the toothpaste he had used. My toothpaste! she thought, and looked at her toothbrush, but there was now a second brush in the mug beside her own. At least he had used his own toothbrush.

It was like a trip back to the past. How often had she gone into a steamy bathroom and gone around picking up after him, tidying, putting things away? Sean's mother must have spoilt him when he was a child, waited on him hand and foot, so that he now seemed to believe that a magic fairy followed him around and did everything for him. When they were married, Nadine had been cast as that magic fairy, but she wasn't playing that role again.

Who had been doing it since she left? she wondered as she stepped under the shower. Fenella? Nadine couldn't believe that. Fenella Nash did not have a domesticated look.

The cool water refreshed her. She felt much better as she began to towel herself afterwards. She dressed quickly before going back into the bedroom in a peach cotton top and matching shorts, her chestnut hair looped back from her face in two coils tied with black ribbon.

Sean hadn't left, of course. She pretended to be surprised about that, though, halting and staring at him.

'I thought I told you to go.'

'I've rung and ordered breakfast,' he told her, setting out the table and chairs on the balcony in preparation for the meal.

She seethed. 'Oh, have you? Well, you aren't staying to eat it!'

'Yes, I am, I'm starving,' he said coolly. 'I told them to send scrambled eggs and mushrooms for me, with toast, and I ordered croissants, rolls, honey and fruit for you, and fruit juice and coffee for both of us.' He gave her a wicked grin. 'See how well I remember what you like for breakfast?'

'You can eat in the dining-room! You aren't eating with me. And take your toothbrush with you, and your case.'

'I'll find myself a room later today,' he told her just as the room service waiter arrived pushing a table laid with breakfast. Calmly, Sean told him to unload the food on to the balcony table, tipped him when the man had finished, and sat down to take the silver cover off his plate of eggs and mushrooms.

'Mmm... delicious!' He took a piece of golden toast and began to eat, and, since Nadine was suddenly forced to realise how hungry she was herself, she sat down opposite him, a little sulkily, poured herself some pineapple juice and took some fruit from the bowl.

'I shall be going to my first class in half an hour,' she told Sean. 'By the time I get back at lunchtime I shall expect you to be out of here.'

'Pour me some coffee, would you, darling?' was his only answer. 'These are the best scrambled eggs I've eaten in years.'

'Sean, I'm serious!' she furiously snapped and he lifted his dark head to look at her, those blue eyes hard and bright.

'I'm not leaving until we've talked.'

She nodded slowly, her face coldly cynical. 'Oh, I know why you're here! Larry told me all about your financial difficulties...'

Sean frowned blackly. 'Oh, did he? Damn him, he had no right... Did he ask you to lend us money?'

'Obliquely, yes. And I know that's why you're here. Well, I'm ready to discuss some sort of loan but not here, not now. I'm on holiday and...'

'It isn't,' Sean interrupted curtly and Nadine stopped talking, staring at him incredulously.

'What?'

'I'm not here to ask you for money!'

'But Larry said...'

'Yes, *Larry* wants you to lend the company money, but I don't. Are you going to pour me that coffee or not?' He forked some soft creamy egg into his mouth while she watched him in disbelief.

'You don't?' she slowly repeated.

He sighed and picked up the coffee-pot, poured them both a cup of the fragrant, dark liquid.

'You don't want me to give you back the divorce settlement money?' Nadine had to clarify the position; she simply couldn't believe what he was saying.

Sean nodded and ate some more egg and mushroom, bit into crisp toast, then took a sip of coffee.

'Sean!' she angrily said. 'I asked you...'

'I heard,' he said, looking up then, his face cool. 'I just told you. I do not want your money. OK?'

She stared into those dangerous blue eyes. 'Then why are you here?'

He smiled crookedly. 'Something you said to Larry made me come.'

She was thrown into a panic, hunting through her memory and getting very confused. 'What? What did I say to Larry?'

'You said that you weren't involved with Jamie Colbert before the divorce, that we split up because of Fenella.'

She stiffened. 'Well, it's true, isn't it?'

'No, it isn't,' Sean said. 'I never so much as looked at Fenella while I was married to you. We were in trouble before I even met Fenella, and the cause of our rows was Colbert. So that's why I'm here—to ask you if you were lying to Larry, or if I was wrong all those years, and you weren't having an affair with Jamie Colbert while we were married.'

CHAPTER FOUR

'I'M NOT getting into another of those endless fights,' Nadine said huskily. 'I still have nightmares about them. You wouldn't believe me then, and I don't expect you to believe me now. It doesn't matter anyway, we're not married anymore, we're divorced—so what's the point of talking about it? Look, I'm going to my art class. Don't be here when I get back, Sean, or I'll pack and leave myself.'

She got up and collected the large blue beach-bag in which she was going to carry all her art things around. Sean still sat on the balcony, drinking his coffee and watching her, his brooding blue eyes narrowed. It wasn't easy to ignore his stare, but she managed it out of sheer practice. Nadine was used to men staring at her, their eyes exploring her from head to foot, from her smooth-skinned face with its wide, passionate mouth, and the coils of rich chestnut hair framing it, down over her high, round breasts and slim waist to her rounded, feminine hips and long, slim, tapering legs. She had had to learn not to blush or get angry; her profession demanded it. She still didn't like it. And when it was Sean doing the watching it was ten times harder for her to stay cool.

She left without saying a word and hurried off to meet the other art students in the lobby of the hotel. Luc then led them through the gardens to his studio, which adjoined the hotel on the left side.

Luc's studio was a spacious room with full-length windows flooding it with light. There were wonderful views on three sides: the gardens, the beach, the blue Caribbean. The fourth wall was stacked with canvases leaning against each other; above them other paintings hung, crammed close together, all Luc's work. Nadine saw water-colours, oils, sketches in charcoal, crayon, pencil: most of them landscapes, a few portraits.

The students were all allotted an easel; Luc told them they were going to do some preparatory sketches of whichever view they were facing, so that he could assess the standard of their work. Some were total beginners, others had been painting for years. His approach to each would necessarily be quite different.

Nadine was so distracted this morning, half her mind still involved in argument with Sean, that she had a problem trying to decide what to draw, and she knew she wasn't doing anything inspired, blocking in the beach, palm trees, bougainvillaea, the brilliant blue sea and sky. It all looked overcoloured suddenly: a picture for a chocolate-box lid. She scowled at it; how did you sketch a view that was all colour? She heard Luc's voice talking to a dark girl in a scarlet sundress who was standing at the next easel.

'Had you thought of putting in a human figure there to give it a focus? You know, when people look at a picture they automatically look first at any human beings in it. It's instinctive...' His voice dropped to a murmur, and Nadine couldn't hear the rest of the sentence.

She looked at her own sketch. There were no human beings in her picture, either. She looked up at the actual view and saw children running under the palm trees, throwing a ball to each other. She began to put them into the picture: nothing elaborate, just blurs in the shadow of the palms.

Luc came up behind her a few moments later; she waited rather nervously for his comment.

'Not bad,' he said, to her surprise. 'You have an eye for perspective. But a little more boldness wouldn't hurt. Be more assertive with form; make it a positive statement, not a nervous little wiggle.' He had a piece of charcoal in his hand and bent forward. 'Like this...' He made a slashing stroke and a palm tree appeared. 'And here, maybe...' Another stroke and there was a man walking on the beach. 'Do you see what I mean?'

'Yes,' she said, envying him that sureness and speed. She was always hesitant to put a line on the paper.

'Take risks, Nadine,' he said, as if he had read her thoughts. 'Start again, and this time don't be scared, be bolder.' He smiled at her encouragingly, then went on to the next student.

Nadine obediently began again, concentrating on her work so fiercely that she forgot Sean, forgot the others in the room, Luc talking to another student, the sound of the sea. All she thought about was what she was doing.

When Luc clapped his hands she almost jumped out of her skin. He was standing in front of the class now. 'Time to break!' he told them all cheerfully. 'I don't know about you but I'm starving, and I happen to know it's a very good lunch today: my wife is serving local crabs stuffed with peppers and herbs, and there's a gorgeous crab gumbo...'

'What's a gumbo?' asked the dark girl next to Nadine, and Luc grinned at her.

'Something between a thick soup and a stew. Quite hot, made with a lot of garlic and hot peppers, and spices and herbs. I love it, but it can be an acquired taste. If you like curry, you'll probably like gumbo. And I expect my wife will have made peas and rice, that's usually on the menu. It's one of the most famous Jamaican dishes, but my wife grew up there, so she likes to cook it. There'll be a selection of salads for the less adventurous among you, and the vegetarians have their own menu, too. But take my advice, try one of our local dishes. I can guarantee you'll love them.'

Nadine went back to her room before lunch, tense as she unlocked the door, half expecting to find Sean there waiting for her. The suite was empty, though, and immaculate; the maids had cleaned it and there was no sign of Sean or his luggage. Even his toothbrush had vanished from the bathroom.

She should have felt relieved, much happier. But she didn't. She felt faintly depressed instead. She looked at herself in the bathroom mirror, grimacing at her pallor and the dullness of her eyes. She was tired, that was all! Her sudden depression had nothing to do with Sean. Nothing at all.

She still continued to brood over him as she washed and changed out of her shorts and top, put on a brief yellow tunic dress. Had he left the hotel, or left the island altogether? Had he found somewhere else to stay?

She brushed her hair out, put on a light foundation cream, a touch of lipstick, before going down to the long terrace which ran behind the hotel. Tables were set out there, under a bamboo roof, through which the sunlight filtered, leaving a slatted pattern of shadow.

She seemed to be the last one down; all her fellow students were seated already and Nadine looked around for a free chair.

Luc beckoned. 'We've kept a place for you here, Nadine! Next to your husband.'

She froze, seeing the all too familiar bronzed face, meeting Sean's mocking blue eyes. So he hadn't left either the island or the hotel! Had he been able to get a room in the hotel? And if so, what on earth had he told Luc Haines? What excuse had he given for not sharing her room? Or was he still planning to share it? Well, he could think again if he was! She was not sharing a bed with him again. She would rather take the next plane back to England.

'Here you are,' he insisted, getting up and holding back the chair next to his own. 'Sit down, Nadine. I can recommend the crab salad, it's the best crab I've ever eaten, and the salad is positively inspired.'

With everyone watching her she had no option. She sat down, but gave Sean a bitter look from under her lowered lashes. If he thought he had her beaten he was going to find out just how wrong he was!

He caught her hidden glance and his mouth twitched. He leaned over to pour wine into her glass, and she was intensely aware of the brush of his lean body.

'You look as if you need a drink, darling! You'll like this—a Californian Chardonnay; a nice, crisp white, very refreshing on a hot day like this!'

Nadine snatched up the menu and read it, trembling with a mixture of rage and nerves. She ordered plain grilled fish with salad, and Luc Haines shook his head at her.

'You can eat that anywhere! You mustn't be scared to try something new, Nadine, must she, Sean?'

'She always has been!' Sean shrugged, and Luc gave her a wry look.

'Remember what I was saying to you in class this morning! If you want to learn to paint you've got to be brave, take risks; and that goes for life, too. Now, why don't you have the crab gumbo to start with?'

Infuriated, she said, 'Oh, OK, I'll try the crab gumbo, but then I'll have plain grilled fish, please!'

The waiter grinned at Luc and vanished to the kitchen. Nadine drank some of the white wine. Sean was right: it was refreshing. She watched him sideways; he was eating stuffed crab neatly, with enjoyment.

Luc's voice made her jump. 'Naughty Nadine,' he said wickedly. 'Now we know why you didn't want to tell us anything about yourself. Trying to be incognito, weren't you? Well, we forgive you—it must be quite a trial being the wife of such a famous man. I'm afraid the secret was out as soon as Sean met my wife this morning. She's a big film buff and a big fan of his films; she could hardly speak when she saw Sean walking across Reception this morning.'

'Your wife is a honey,' Sean said. 'Lucky for us that she's a film buff, Nadine—she was able to give us a second room, next door to the suite...'

Nadine tensed, turning a pair of glittering, angry eyes on him, and Sean gave her a sunny smile.

'She was quite horrified when I explained how often I would have to make phone calls in the middle of the night, which usually meant waking you up too. This time difference is a nuisance, but in my business the telephone is a lifeline. And Clarrie Haines was good enough to get me this other room.'

'One of our American guests is leaving tonight,' Luc told her cheerfully. 'Sean can have the room as soon as it has been cleaned. We'll get that done by eight. So you won't be kept awake tonight with Sean's international phone calls.'

'Isn't that wonderful news, darling?' Sean asked softly.

'Wonderful,' she said, smiling although her jaws were aching with the effort not to scream. How did he do it? He always got his own way somehow—that was what made him such a great film producer and director. Whenever he met an obstacle he managed to get over it, whatever the cost to himself and everyone around him.

It was a relief when her crab gumbo arrived and she could turn her attention to the food. As Luc had promised, it was hot and spicy, and the crab was the best she had ever eaten. While she ate Luc and Sean talked and the other guests listened with obvious fascination.

They weren't talking about films, though; they were involved in a long discussion about painters. Sean had a small collection of modern art: a Picasso sketch given to him by a French actor for his birthday years ago, a Lowry he had bought himself, a Beryl Cook painting of her usual plump ladies, this time playing tennis on a summer day, their white outfits dazzling against the dark green of bushes and trees.

'Nadine gave me that,' Sean said, the flick of his eyes making her heart skip as she remembered the occasion. It had been Christmas Day four years ago; they had got up late and drunk buck's fizz while they opened their presents under the tree. She had given him the Beryl Cook picture: he had given her the most breathtaking emerald earrings.

'Put them on now,' he had said huskily, and taken her back to bed to make love, still wearing them and only them.

She knew he was remembering it too, and her cheeks burnt under his gaze.

'This afternoon you must look round my studio,' Luc said with that wicked look she was beginning to recognise. He enjoyed coat-trailing, teasing, being provocative. 'Maybe you'll see something of mine you like. You can't have a good modern collection without one of mine!'

'I already have two of your water-colours,' said Sean, and Luc looked genuinely surprised.

'Really? Which? When did you buy them?'

'I bought one of them at your London exhibition four years ago: a painting of a harbour, done on the island, here, I imagine. The other is a painting of a West Indian market which Nadine gave me years ago—that's my favourite, I love the blindingly bright colours. On a rainy grey morning in London they can lift my whole day.'

Luc smiled with pleasure. 'Glad to hear it! I'd hate to live in London, I love the sun too much. I've often painted the market—it always gives me a good picture. I suppose painting and film making are very similar. We're both after the same thing.'

Sean nodded. 'Couldn't agree more. In fact, we start with a story-board, of course: each little sketch one frame of the film, showing how the story will move along, what it will look like.'

'Fascinating,' Luc said. 'I'd love to come along some day and watch you working, or does it put you off to have visitors on the set?'

'Not at all. Let me know in advance and I'll fix it for you.'

'Thanks,' said Luc with warmth, caught Nadine's cool gaze and asked, 'Do you act, Nadine?'

'No,' she said curtly and Sean made a wry face.

'Ouch. That's a tender spot you touched, Luc. She wanted to act, but...'

'But I can't!' she finished for him and stood up. She had finished her grilled fish, and everyone else was already eating a dessert, mostly local fruit. 'I don't want a dessert, I have things to do, excuse me.'

She hurried back into the hotel to her room before Sean could catch up with her. After locking the door she changed into a swimsuit, tied a filmy beach-wrap around her, put a book and a Walkman with headphones into her beach-bag, and went off to the beach. There were no more classes that afternoon; everyone was free to do as they liked and what Nadine wanted to do was lie in the sun, listen to music and relax.

The hotel's beach was private, and, when she arrived, empty. The blue Caribbean waters tumbled on to the silvery sands with a restful murmur, the sun was high and hot, the horizon shimmered. Nadine moved one of the hotel's loungers under the shade of a large striped umbrella, set her bag down on a low plastic table beside her and sat down, her head on her bent knees, staring at the sea, listening to gulls crying overhead, watching some black and white waders moving along the beach, their long, curved beaks digging deep into the fine sand.

She gave a sigh, and untied her beach-wrap, stood up and hung it carefully from the ribs of the umbrella so that it gently blew to and fro over her, like a lace curtain in the faint breeze coming off the sea. Sitting down again, she got a bottle of suntan lotion from her bag and began to use it on her legs.

'Need some help?'

The cool voice made her jump. She almost dropped the bottle of lotion as her head swung to face Sean.

He was practically naked, just wearing black sunglasses with mirror lenses which reflected the sun back at the sky, and black silky briefs which deepened his golden tan and made his long legs look even longer. Nadine looked away, swallowing, a pulse beating hard in her throat.

'Did you have to come down here? Why can't you leave me alone? I wanted a couple of hours' peace, and you're going to ruin the whole afternoon.' She put the cap back on to the bottle of lotion. Sean reached for it. 'Leave it alone!' said Nadine furiously, but he pulled it out of her hand and unscrewed the cap again.

'I'll do your back—turn over.'

'No.' Her face was mutinous. He was beginning to make her really angry: arriving out of the blue, wrecking her holiday, refusing to leave, and now coming down here and destroying the blissful silence of the golden afternoon.

Sean put the bottle down on the sand and knelt beside her on the lounger, his bare legs brushing hers. She gave a gasp of shock.

'Don't you touch me!'

He looked down at her through those shielding lenses and she wished she could see his eyes. 'You don't want to get sunburn and that sun is very hot.' He poured glistening oil into his palm and Nadine's mouth went dry.

'I can put it on myself!' She tried to sit up and he pushed her back with one peremptory hand, and with the other began to smooth the oil into her bare shoulders, his fingers sensitive, cool, following her bone-structure, the roundness before her arm began, the line from there to her neck, sliding down into the hollows between bones, up along her throat.

Nadine felt boneless, weak; she watched him from under her lashes, intensely aware of everything around them, the sound of the sea, the cry of the seabirds, the burning blue of the afternoon sky. Sean slid the straps of her swimsuit down and an alarm bell went off in her head.

'Stop that!' she bit out, struggled to get up and found herself inches away from him, their bodies so close you couldn't get a hand between them, his face unreadable, the mirrored glasses flashing in the sunlight, the hard, passionate mouth parted—smiling or sighing?

'You're still the sexiest woman I've ever met,' he whispered, and suddenly bent his head and kissed her naked breast.

Nadine almost fainted. She couldn't breathe, she couldn't move; she closed her eyes and felt the soft touch of his mouth with an intensity that made her shake.

Sean's arms went round her, his head lifted abruptly, and his mouth took hers with a burning demand that made her head spin. His body pushed against hers until she fell back and he fell with her, kissing her fiercely, hungrily, lying on top of her, their legs twining, naked bodies sensually restless as they moved against each other. Nadine wanted him so badly that she forgot everything else, all her reasons for being angry with him, for distrusting him. There was only one thing on her mind, on both their minds.

Until she heard the voices. They broke into her yielding mood, tore up the sun and silence of the afternoon.

Stiffening, she broke off the kiss, pushed Sean away and he sat up, flushed and breathing thickly, staring away from her, across the silver sands, towards the hotel gardens. Some other guests were wandering down to the beach, under the palm trees, talking and laughing.

Nadine sat up, pushed the straps of her swimsuit back into place, straightened her tumbled chestnut hair.

'Go away and leave me alone!' she hissed at Sean, who looked back at her, his mouth twisting in sardonic comprehension of her changed mood.

He didn't bother to answer; just stood up, raking back his hair, moved another lounger under the shade of the umbrella next to her and spread his towel over it before lying down, the dark glasses still firmly in place on his nose above that arrogant mouth.

Nadine hesitated between ignoring him and leaving, going back to the hotel. But that would be running away; Sean had already won their last little skirmish, and she wasn't going to let him win every battle, however much it cost her.

She lay down, hunted for her own sunglasses, put them on. She got out her Walkman, dropped in a tape of her current favourite group and opened her paperback book.

She was reading a new detective story by one of her favourite authors: it was hard to concentrate, though; the turns and twists of the plot seemed to make little sense, and she couldn't remember who all the characters were because her mind was pre-occupied with other things. With Sean. With her own weak, stupid feelings for him. She kept re-membering the last months of their marriage: the loneliness and bitterness she had felt. He'd so rarely been there, and when he was all they did was quarrel. She'd known he was seeing Fenella Nash, he had talked about her all the time, to everyone: friends, the Press, people he worked with. He'd been obsessed with her. He thought Fenella was the find of the century: the camera loved her, she was beautiful, she could act almost without moving a muscle. One flicker of her long black lashes and she conveyed oceans of meaning, Sean had said, smiling, and Nadine had listened, sick with jealousy.

And whenever they were alone he was edgy and irritable, picking rows over nothing, seeming eager to get away from her again. Their marriage had been in trouble long before they finally split apart, and whatever Sean might say now it had been because of him and Fenella, not because he was jealous over Jamie. She had been working with Jamie for years. Sean had never liked him much, and admittedly he had often said he wished she wouldn't work with Jamie so often, but then Sean didn't want her to work at all. He wanted her to give up modelling, he didn't see why she wanted to have a career when she was his wife—that should be enough for her. He wanted her to have his baby, start a family.

She had wanted children. One day. But she knew that once she had a baby her body would change drastically, even after the birth, even if she lost all the weight she had necessarily gained during pregnancy. Her breasts would be fuller, less firm, her stomach not so flat, she was terrified of getting stretch marks, of not being able to recover her elasticity, the suppleness and muscle-tone she had. She had seen it happen to other girls in her profession and it spelt the end for them.

She was getting quite old for modelling, anyway: once you were in your twenties you were on the slow slide from the top. There were always young girls coming up to get the best jobs. She had wanted to have a few more years before she had to stop but Sean wouldn't listen when she explained; he seemed to resent her career too much.

Maybe that had been the real cause of their broken marriage? she thought bleakly, closing her eyes. Maybe Fenella and Jamie had only been the excuses they used for having quarrels which were really about something else entirely. A sigh wrenched her. What was the point of this endless searching for reasons? Why keep going over the past? Their marriage was finished. She ought to be getting on with her life.

Their marriage, maybe, she thought grimly. But not, she had to face now, the way she felt about Sean. That wasn't finished. She wasn't over him. She wished to God she were. The sexual chemistry exploded between them every time he was near her. She felt it even now, when they were lying side by side on this beach, not even looking at each other let alone touching; not even alone, come to that.

There were quite a few people on the beach now; she heard them vaguely through the insistent beat of her music. There was a party of young people, not students from her class, but obviously staying in the hotel. They were bronzed and fit: she watched them running down the sand, splashing into the blue Caribbean, chucking a beach-ball high into the air from one to the other. As she watched them they became aware of her, openly staring at her curved, very female figure in the clinging jade-green swimsuit, and Nadine quickly looked away, pretended to be unaware of them.

Sean didn't, however. She picked up tension from him; he was watching the other men, his face hard, forbidding, set in silent antagonism. That was how he had always reacted when other men stared at her. He meant to scare them off—and usually did.

He did now. The tanned youngsters turned away hurriedly, and she saw them swimming out to a raft which was tethered in the sea just off the beach. Nadine almost laughed. If she hadn't been so irritated she would have done. She didn't blame them. Any sane person would run away from Sean when he looked like that. He had an air of threat, of danger: it was the brooding look in those blue eyes, the muscled power of that lean body. Even lying on a lounger on the beach he disturbed, the way a black panther disturbed when it stretched out in the sun, apparently at rest but always tensely waiting to make its kill.

The sun was now too hot for her. She shifted her position, moved into deeper shadow under the umbrella. Her book fell to the sand. She yawned, eyelids heavy, and gradually drifted off to sleep, into dreams. Dreams of Sean, of his body against her, his mouth on hers, his hands silkily exploring, making her burn and twist hungrily closer.

She woke up with a start, trembling; opened her eyes and found herself looking straight into Sean's watchful blue stare. He was lying on his side, his lounger so close that he was almost touching her. He had been watching her while she slept. Heat swept up Nadine's face. He couldn't know what she had been dreaming about, yet she blushed, as if he could, wondering anxiously if she had made any betraying movements, sounds, while she dreamt. She hadn't said anything, had she?

His intense stare made her heart begin to beat thickly, suffocatingly. She couldn't bear it. She jumped up and began to run, down to the sea, across the hot sands. The water was cool and delicious on her sun-flushed skin as she began to swim. There was nobody on the raft any more so she made for that, and climbed up on to it to rest for a moment, only to realise as she heaved herself out of the water that Sean had followed her, was close behind her.

He climbed up on to the raft too, in an effortless lunge, shaking the water from his black hair, his tanned skin glistening as he sat down beside her, his long legs dangling in the blue Caribbean, one brown, wet thigh almost touching her.

She was far too aware of that contact and that made her violently angry. She turned on him, her eyes blazing.

'Why won't you leave me alone? You're ruining my holiday, and it's the first I've had in ages. I really need this break, I'm tired after months of hard work, and when I go back I'll have to face all the stress of starting a new career, and an even more difficult one. The next year is going to be a tremendous strain. If I'm going to make a success on TV I'll need to give it everything I've got, which is why I need this holiday. I'm not asking for much—just a little peace and quiet! But I'm not getting it with you around. If you don't go, I'll have to leave! And you're wasting your time, anyway. Whatever it is you're after, you're not getting it. You and I are finished. Get that into your head!'

He had listened at first with a lazy, mocking smile, but after her first few words his face changed, tightened, reflected an anger just as great as hers.

'We aren't finished, Nadine!' he threw back at her, his voice harsh. 'Not until I say so!'

'You did say so,' she bitterly reminded him. 'We got divorced, remember!'

'Words,' he bit out. 'Just words on paper, a lot of legal babble. Whatever the law says, the truth is we're still connected, Nadine; there's a chain binding us and it hasn't broken.' He put his hand on her thigh and she jumped, stiffening tensely.

'Don't!'

Sean was watching her, his hard mouth curling in sardonic comment on her reaction. 'Yes. You feel it. I feel it. Whether I'm touching you or not, whether I'm even with you or not, we're still connected, still linked.' His voice dropped, deepened, murmuring huskily. 'We're one flesh, Nadine. I'm only just beginning to understand what that means...'

'Stop it!' she cried out fiercely, shaking. 'I am not sleeping with you! Leave me alone!'

She meant to dive back into the water but Sean moved faster. One minute she was sitting on the edge of the raft, poised to leap into the blue Caribbean, the next her shoulders were pinned to the wood; and she was looking up at Sean as he knelt above her, his knees clamping her waist.

Nadine was speechless, her heart crashing against her ribs. His dark head blotted out the world, riveted her dazed eyes.

'I want to try again, Nadine,' he said, and she couldn't breathe. 'We had something special. Didn't we? It went wrong, I'm not even sure why, and I don't think you are. It was perfect, yet it all fell apart without rhyme or reason; we kept having those terrible quarrels and they poisoned everything. You said just now that it's finished between us, but you know you were lying. It isn't over, far from it. There's still something very powerful between us, and I want a last chance to get it all back, whatever we had. OK, it may be too late to retrieve what we had in the beginning, but maybe we can build something new on the ruins.'

He stopped, gave a short, wrenched sigh and looked down into her hazel eyes, his mouth shakily half smiling. 'Will you try again, Nadine?'

Nadine stared back at him, trying to think; her body, her senses, her heart, clamouring hungrily for him, fighting on his side, as they always had from the moment she met him. Her mind was confused and uncertain. She couldn't deny that their sexual chemistry was as potent as ever, but sex was only one part of a relationship between a man and a woman. What about the rest? She couldn't bear to get locked into that bitter private war again.

She looked away, biting her lip, stared into the shimmering, halcyon blue sky. What was she to do?

CHAPTER FIVE

'SAY something, Nadine!' Sean's voice grated with tension and she gave a long sigh.

'I need time to think! You can't just come out with something like that out of the blue and expect me to give an off-the-cuff answer. Give me time to think about it!'

'How much time do you need?'

'I don't know! As long as it takes for me to work out what I want...'

'You know what you want,' he said thickly, and her pulses went crazy at the way he was looking at her. 'We both want the same thing. I don't know about you, but I'm going out of my mind with frustration.'

So was she, especially at this moment, with him kneeling over her, his thighs warm against her, his hands restlessly shifting on her arms as though they wanted to wander elsewhere. Sean had a dynamic sexuality: he was the most intensely male man she had ever known, his masculinity like the heat of the sun, the crash of the waves, a natural force of which you could never be unaware and which you couldn't fight.

'Our marriage turned into a war!' she cried out in something approaching desperation. 'I don't know if I can stand the strain of trying again...'

'I'm not asking you to marry me again,' Sean said quickly, and she looked at him in confusion, bewildered.

'What? You just said...you wanted to try again...'

He shrugged, his face wry. 'We've tried marriage and, as you say, it didn't work; we ended up at each other's throats. Why don't we just have an affair?'

Nadine was dumbstruck. She stared at him, her mouth open, her hazel eyes huge.

Sean began to laugh, wicked amusement in his voice. 'Your face, darling! You look quite shocked!'

'Not shocked,' she muttered. 'Just...taken aback...'

'Why? It won't be the first affair you've ever had, will it? Queen Victoria died a long time ago. We're both adults, and you can't tell me you've been sleeping alone since we split up!'

Her eyes slid away; she flushed, and heard his sudden rough intake of breath.

'Tell me the truth, Nadine,' he broke out, his voice harsh. 'Have you slept with anyone else? What about Colbert?'

She flared up then, glaring at him. 'How many times do I have to tell you? Jamie and I never had an affair, either while I was married to you or after we split up! I told you that a hundred times—but you wouldn't believe me. I don't suppose there's any point in telling you again, but for the last time: Jamie's a friend, I'm fond of him, but that's all there is to it. Basically we're colleagues who work well together, and respect each other.'

Sean was watching her narrowly, his face pale and set. 'He's mad about you, Nadine! I've seen the way he looks at you and...'

'Oh, stop it!' she yelled, close to breaking point. 'You say you want to try again, but even before we start you're harping on the same old theme—what's the point?' She gave him a violent push and Sean went sprawling backwards, tumbled into the ocean with a loud splash and sank like a stone.

Nadine knelt anxiously on the side of the raft for a second, watching until she saw his body rising up again through the sunlit blue water. He was thrashing his arms, coughing, his black hair slicked down, seal-like, on his head.

Once she knew he wasn't in trouble, she dived in too, from the side of the raft closest to shore, and began to swim strongly towards the silvery sands, her chestnut hair streaming behind her on the surface.

Sean would have heard the splash as she dived in but he was on the far side of the raft and it took him a moment or two to swim round the raft before he could follow her. He was a stronger swimmer than her, though; she soon heard him cleaving the water far too close behind her. She used up her last remaining energy in a burst of speed to make sure she reached the beach before he caught up with her.

As she waded up the sands, wringing out her hair, which was so wet its colour had darkened almost to black, Luc Haines waved to her from the beach bar which had now opened at the edge of the beach closest to the hotel gardens.

'Nadine! So there you are! We've been looking everywhere for you. You've had an urgent phone call from London.' There was something odd in his voice, in the way he was looking at her. 'He said he would ring back in fifteen minutes, so you'll have time to get out of that wet suit and take the call in your room.'

Nadine frowned, taken aback. 'Oh. OK. Thanks.' Why was he looking at her in that quizzical fashion, though? And who on earth could be calling her here? Very few people knew where she was. Her agent, Jamie, Greg Erroll. Nobody else.

'Did you take the name?' she hesitantly asked, half hoping he hadn't because she didn't want anyone here to know too much about her.

'I asked,' Luc said drily. 'He said just to tell you it was Greg.'

'Thank you.' Nadine's flush deepened as she heard Sean coming up out of the water, watching them intently as he shook the water off his hair. She wondered if Greg Erroll had said anything else, had somehow aroused Luc's curiosity. Or wasn't it the phone call that had altered Luc's manner towards her?

'I'd better collect my things, then, and go back to the hotel,' she said, as Sean began to lope across the sand towards them, every movement he made observed eagerly by a group of girls in tiny bikinis sitting at the beach bar counter sipping iced drinks and whispering together. No doubt they had just heard that Sean was a film producer but that didn't entirely explain their fascination with him. It was

Sean's sexual magnetism working again, and Nadine angrily turned away and began stuffing things back into her beach-bag.

Sean strolled over to join her, his silky black briefs clinging wetly to his body, his lean, bronzed body gleaming in the sunlight, drops of salt water caught in the wiry black curls of hair on his chest. Nadine gave him one brief glance then looked away angrily.

'What was Haines saying to you?' he demanded, picking up his towel and beginning to dry himself.

'Greg Erroll has rung and is ringing again in a quarter of an hour,' she informed him, her voice clipped.

'What does he want?' Sean began to frown blackly.

'How do I know? No doubt he'll tell me when he rings back.' Nadine slung her beach-bag over her shoulder and turned away. As she walked past the beach-bar the girls sitting there stared at her, whispering together. She tried not to hear but scraps of words came to her through the hot, still air.

'Nadine Carmichael...she was his wife...no, they're divorced...' Giggle, giggle. 'They're here together...no, really. I heard from my room-maid, they're sleeping together...' A wave of excited giggles followed that and Nadine's lips clamped together; she averted her flushed face angrily. She would have liked to run, to get out of hearing range, but that would have been undignified, would have been some sort of victory for the younger girls, who were enjoying talking about her while she was in earshot. 'No, she's not a film star, silly. She's just a model,' one of them said, raising her voice.

Nadine quickened her step, she was almost out of range. A few scraps of words floated after her. 'Yes, you know her; that TV ad... TV... model... that girl...'

Footsteps grated on the sandy path and she started, looking round. Luc Haines fell into step beside her and gave her a dry sideways look.

'I knew there was something else you weren't telling us. So you're a famous model and appear on TV advertisements!'

She grimly asked, 'How did you find out?'

'A guest recognised you. It was bound to happen sooner or later, obviously, if you're that famous. You must have known that!'

'It seemed so far from here to London, I thought...I hoped...nobody would recognise me.'

He gave her a sudden, sweet smile. 'I'm sorry you were. Is it hell being recognised everywhere you go?'

'I'm used to it in London, but it is tiring, always being on display; it's like living in a shop window. You can never relax or forget people are watching you.'

He nodded. 'And so you wanted to get away from it all, just for a couple of weeks! I can understand that. I'm sorry you've been spotted!'

They had reached the hotel lobby. Nadine gave him a rueful little smile. 'Oh, well, I'm used to it.'

Abruptly Luc asked, 'Will you let me paint you?'

She looked back at him steadily. 'I'm a very expensive model.'

Luc laughed and so did she, but it was a faintly bitter amusement she felt and Luc watched her face as if reading her response, and frowned.

'I wanted to paint you before I knew who you were,' he reminded her. 'The first time we met I asked if I could paint you. Remember?'

She nodded slowly, remembering; and then thought that she rather liked the idea of being painted by such a good artist.

'Just so long as you don't expect me to take my clothes off,' she half joked.

He shook his head. 'It's your face I'm interested in, not your body.'

'Well, that's a novel approach!' said a cold voice behind them, and Nadine stiffened, her hazel eyes widening in shock.

She had been so absorbed in her conversation with Luc that she hadn't noticed Sean's arrival. He was standing right behind them, his brooding blue eyes fixed on her face in a ruthless dissection of her feelings which was only too bleakly familiar to her. Sean had always been a jealous, possessive man who resented seeing any other men with her, and he obviously didn't believe Luc's claim to be interested in her face rather than her body. What he was trying to guess was whether or not she was interested in Luc, and Nadine resented that probing stare.

She turned on her heel and walked away from both men. If Sean wanted to pick a fight he could do it without her as an audience; she had had enough for one day.

She carefully locked her door and closed the blinds at the windows before she stripped and took a rapid shower. Just as she was towelling her wet hair the phone rang and she ran to pick it up.

'Nadine? It's Greg!'

'Hello, Greg,' she said, curling up on her bed, wrapped in her towelling robe. 'Is anything wrong?'

'Far from it!' he said in a warm, friendly voice. 'The media stuff you did before you left is all out now and we're very pleased with the impact you made. Congratulations. Are you having a good holiday?'

She grimaced, glad he couldn't see her face. 'Yes, thanks.' Apart from the presence of my maddening ex-husband! she thought grimly, but she certainly wasn't confiding that news to Greg Erroll. The fewer people who knew that Sean had followed her out here the better. She was already having night-mares in case the Press got hold of the story. She could just imagine the headlines and she flinched at the thought of what they were likely to say.

'Good,' Greg said briskly. 'Would it be a terrible bore to interrupt it?'

'Interrupt it?' she repeated in disbelief. She might have known! No, come on—she *had* known! From the minute Luc told her that Greg had rung she had begun to suspect something. Greg Erroll wouldn't have rung her here just to ask if she was having a good time on holiday. He had to have a very serious reason for this call.

'Just for a few days,' he quickly added.

'To do what?'

'I wouldn't ask you if it wasn't something very special,' he coaxed.

'Come out with it, Greg, don't be devious,' Nadine groaned.

He laughed. 'It's a TV appearance, in the States—in Miami, in fact. They picked up on you from the British Press coverage, and they want you to do a chat show on Friday night. I wouldn't ask you to interrupt your holiday if it was anywhere else, but Miami isn't a difficult trip from where you are! I could have a private plane pick you up, fly you to Miami, to do the show, and afterwards you could spend the night at a hotel . . . there's a very good one right next to the airport, the Sheraton River House, or you could stay at the Grand Bay, which is in Coconut Grove; that's where I always stay when I'm in Miami. The hotel has the most amazing views over the bay, and I love the food they serve. You might like to spend a couple of days shopping in Miami before you go back. Have you been there? The shopping is terrific.'

She was thinking hard. 'Friday? Would the plane pick me up on Friday?'

'Yes, in the morning, preferably, to give you time to acclimatise, settle down before the show in the evening. Miami is probably a little more humid than where you are. I always find that area of the West Indies rather windy.'

'It's gorgeous at the moment,' she said absently. 'But I gather that they do have some very strong winds and quite a bit of rain in early spring.'

'I obviously pick the wrong time of year.' There was a little silence then Greg asked, 'Well? Will you do it?'

'Yes, I'll do it.'

The warmth in his voice increased. Greg liked people to do what he wanted them to do; it made him like them more.

'Good girl. Now, will you want to fly straight back next day, or stay in Miami for a few days?'

'I'll stay for a couple of days, I think,' she told him, and he laughed.

'I guessed you wouldn't be able to resist the shopping idea! OK, I'll arrange everything for you and be in touch to let you know the details.'

She hung up a moment later and lay back on the bed, her arms behind her head. She didn't really want to go to Miami, but it was a heaven-sent opportunity to get away from Sean for a while. She wasn't even sure she would come back here. She might fly to London instead. The whole idea of this holiday had been to get away from her problems back home, but Sean had brought them here with him, and she knew she wouldn't be able to concentrate on her painting lessons while Sean was prowling around, disturbing her with his talk of affairs and trying again.

She had been tempted. Why try to deny it? She closed her eyes, shivering convulsively. Oh, yes, she had been tempted; the suggestion had sent a wave of desire crashing through her. But she mustn't be so weak; she had to remember all the reasons why she must not let Sean talk her into anything so disastrous.

She couldn't face getting hurt again, and theirs had always been an explosive relationship; what chance was there that either of them had changed in the time apart?

Their careers had kept them apart so much, and even when they were together there had been constant friction. Sean was jealous of every man she ever met, especially Jamie Colbert, of course. He couldn't believe that Jamie didn't want to be her lover, wasn't in love with her.

She sighed, her hazel eyes wry. And it was true, in a way. Jamie was in love with her. But only in the same sense that he loved every girl he photographed. Jamie loved what he saw in his camera's lens: he used his camera to freeze time, catch a woman like a flower, at her most lovely, preserve her for eternity. It was a drive for power, in a way; he wanted to control what the camera looked at, arrange the woman, her clothes, her background, and then fix it for ever.

Jamie's love for her was not personal, not particular, but Sean would never believe that. He wanted her himself, so he assumed that Jamie must. His jealousy had not been rational, and neither had her own.

Because she had been jealous, too; she didn't deny it. How could she help being jealous of all those lovely women in the film business who pursued him night and day in the hope of getting a big part in one of his films? She hadn't had to descend to those tactics to get on in her career, but she knew plenty of girls who had, who were eager to offer themselves to any man who could be useful to them, and Sean himself had told her often enough about passes which had been made at him by ambitious girls. Before they'd met he had had a whole string of girlfriends, although none of them had lasted for long. Sean had once had a very wild reputation. Nadine knew that she had had far better reasons for being jealous over him than he had ever had for being jealous over her.

And, even if their relationship had survived the long partings, the jealousy and suspicion that kept poisoning their love, they would still have been torn apart by Sean's angry demands that she give up her career to have a baby. She could never forget the way he had refused to listen to her, refused to try to understand her point of view.

He would not have given up his entire career in order to have a baby, she had kept saying. Why should she?

'Oh, don't be ridiculous, it's not the same at all,' he'd growled. 'I'm a man, I can't have babies. You're a woman; having babies is what nature intended you for!'

'And nothing else, I suppose!' she had flared, hardly believing he had said such a thing, sounding as if he meant every word of it, too.

'Well, you do have other uses,' Sean had said, and actually laughed, looking at her through his lashes with deliberate sensuality.

'Don't treat me like this, Sean!' she had burst out, so angry her voice had shaken. 'You sound like Valentino! Well, you're no desert sheikh and I don't have the harem mentality. How dare you say I have my uses?'

'Oh, don't be ridiculous, it was a joke!' he had snapped back, scowling.

'Some joke! It doesn't make me laugh.'

'You never have had a sense of humour!' he had growled, looking at her as if he didn't even like her, let alone love her. 'What's the matter with you these days? We used to be able to talk to each other, we laughed at the same jokes once, but lately every time I say a word you bite my head off!'

She had been taken aback by that accusation and looked at him uncertainly, wondering, Was that true? A sense of desolation had swept over her, a sense of helplessness. They were being pulled apart remorselessly and she didn't know how to stop it. She only knew she loved him and she didn't want to lose him, yet at the same time she was not prepared to let him dictate what she did with her life.

A little more gently she had tried to explain herself to him. 'Look, Sean, I know you want to have a baby, and I want one too, some day, but I have my own agenda, and it doesn't involve having a baby for some years yet. I want to go on modelling while I still can, and then start a new career, with a future. Only after that will I be ready to take some years out to have a baby or two, see them through the first few years, and then go back to work after they've started school.'

'You don't have to stop work for years. You can get a nanny; most career women do!'

'Maybe, but I can't see the point. Why have a baby at all if I'm going to hand it over to some other woman to look after while I go back to work? I might have help with the baby on a part-time basis, to give myself a break, I might even do some part-time work once the baby is two or three, but until I'm ready to be a full-time mother I'm not having a baby at all.'

'You just don't want to have a baby, full stop!' Sean had accused.

'I told you...I do want one, one day, but I'm not ready to do it yet!'

He had given her a grim look. 'If we follow your agenda I'll be in my forties by the time you have a baby! I don't want to wait that long.'

'Well, I'm sorry, but maybe we could work out a compromise...' she had begun, and he had exploded.

'I know your idea of compromise! You mean you get your own way and I accept it!'

'No, that's your idea, not mine. You're the one who's determined to have his own way.'

'When we got married I thought we would be starting a family right away.'

'You didn't tell me that when you asked me to marry you! You didn't tell me you expected me to have a baby right away.'

'I assumed you would want one! We used to talk about having children and you seemed as keen as I was...'

She had remembered then those weekends when they had cuddled up together on the couch in his country cottage, in front of a roaring log fire, and talked dreamily about what they wanted from life. A family had always been part of their dreams.

'I was...' she had whispered, biting her lip. 'I am...'

'Don't lie, Nadine!' he had bitterly said. 'Not any more. You lied to me, then, you cheated me...I thought you were someone very different, I thought I had found the mother of my children, but it turns out that you're just another ambitious woman with her sights set on stardom!'

'That's not true!' She had been bitter, too; and so the quarrel had ended like all their quarrels, like their marriage itself.

They had gone round and round in circles without ever coming to an end, or resolving any of the issues they fought over, and finally they had split apart after one last terrible row. They hadn't talked about divorce at first. They simply could not bear to see each other because it was too painful. The days had become weeks. The weeks had become months. Their lawyers had talked. They hadn't. They were both busy working.

When the word divorce first cropped up it had been a shock for Nadine, but her lawyer had pointed out that it was an inevitable conclusion after such a long separation, and that Sean undoubtedly wanted to marry again, so she had said she wouldn't contest a divorce, and the long process had begun.

She had gone on working and tried to forget how miserable she was by leading a lively social life for a while: partying in London or New York, Rome or the Côte d'Azur, with the international jet-set. As Sean Carmichael's wife her place in their ranks would have been assured, especially as she was known to be very wealthy now, but Nadine was famous in her own right too. Fortune-hunting young men had pursued her; society hostesses had sent her invitations; she was an asset at a party with those famous looks and the glamour her background conferred. For a while she had been the flavour of the month on the international party circuit.

But that life, she found, had palled rapidly. Nadine wasn't the type for wild parties: they made it too hard to get up in the morning and they ruined your complexion, not to mention your health. So she had stopped dashing about from big party to big party, and got back to working hard while she looked around for inspiration for a new career as soon as her modelling had to stop.

It was an empty, lonely existence, in spite of all her friends and colleagues—but it was peaceful and the pain had slowly seeped away. Until a few weeks ago when she walked into Sean in the lobby of the TV studios. One look into those brooding blue eyes and excitement had flared dangerously inside her. Pain had kick-started back into existence; peace had fled. She had had to face the fact that she wasn't over him, and might never get over him. Even more disturbing, Sean knew it, and was ruthlessly prepared to use her weakness against her.

Restlessly she slid off the bed and began to dress for dinner. She put on a sleeveless, vivid yellow summer dress with a full calf-length skirt, a cutaway spider's web design in black and yellow making up the back and a low-cut plunging neckline in the front. Dangling black tassel earrings swung from her ears; she tied her chestnut hair back with a big black satin bow, lightly smoothed foundation over her skin and brushed a little warm coral pink lipstick on to her mouth, dusted her lids with a glittering green eyeshadow.

Her reflection stared back defiantly. She was not going to let Sean guess that she planned to run away from him. She wasn't going to let him monopolise her at dinner tonight, either, or over the days before she caught that plane to Miami. Somehow she would have to think of a way of keeping him at bay—but what?

She went down to dinner a little early, and met Luc Haines and his wife in the bar.

'Well, look at you!' Luc said, his eyes widening as he stared. 'That's a very striking dress!'

'Is it a designer label?' asked Clarrie Haines, and Nadine nodded.

'An English designer,' she said, and told them who had made it.

'Too expensive for you, my love,' Luc told his wife, who grimaced cheerfully.

'I know! I can dream, can't I?'

'Not necessarily,' said Nadine quickly. 'If you're ever in London go to his showroom; he usually has a half-price rack—either second-time-around clothes, brought in by customers who hate wearing the same thing more than a couple of times, or display clothes which have been knocked down in price to get rid of them.'

'Really? I'll certainly check that out next time we're in London,' said Clarrie. 'I really love your dress, though, especially the colours, I don't think I've ever seen that yellow paired up with black, and the full skirt is gorgeous.'

'Give us a twirl!' said Luc, and she laughed, and obeyed, her full skirts swirling around her long, slender legs.

'That back is extraordinary,' Clarrie said. 'Can I have a closer look?'

Nadine obligingly turned her back to Clarrie and found herself facing Sean, who must just have come down for dinner and was lounging against the door frame of the bar staring at her. He was wearing a white evening jacket with a red carnation in his buttonhole and a red silk cummerbund. They stared at each other. Neither smiled, neither spoke. Nadine felt the air between them vibrating with tense awareness.

'Wow!' Clarrie said, one finger tracing the spider's web pattern on Nadine's back. 'Almost sinister, isn't it? Luc, if you paint her, you must get her to wear this dress and try to paint the back view as well as the front—maybe you could have a reflection in a mirror?'

'Mirrors,' Luc said, almost dreamily. 'Yes. But lots of mirrors, I think...yes...Clarrie, you always give me such wonderful ideas, no wonder I adore you. Yes, that's it. I'll paint her in a room full of mirrors, reflections of her everywhere, from all angles, and in the mirrors eyes watching her, men's eyes...'

Nadine shivered and turned pale. 'What a horrible idea!' Across the room her eyes still held Sean's; she saw his narrow and darken.

Luc gave her a dry little smile. 'Well, that's the point, isn't it? Models and actresses are always on show, always being photographed, watched, by men, everywhere you go you're reflected in mirrors, and in men's eyes.' He was thinking aloud, his voice slow and serious. 'In another way, it applies to all women, too, doesn't it? Men watch women all the time and women are always conscious of men watching them; they dress for men, to get their attention—hence the spider's web...'

'I like it,' Clarrie said, eyes wide and shining, she put her arms around him, kissed him, gave him a hug. 'Brilliant, my darling. I always love your symbolist painting.'

'I know you do.'

For a moment they looked at each other with an intimate understanding that shut out Nadine, Sean, everyone else in the room, and Nadine watched them with envy and sadness because that was how her marriage to Sean should have been, a shared warmth, an understanding, a rich intimacy. Instead it had been warfare, because each of them had wanted to make the rules, had wanted the other to submit, she realised. Neither of them would compromise. Marriage couldn't work like that.

Clarrie suddenly looked over Luc's shoulder at the bar clock and gave a little scream.

'Look at the time! I must get back to my kitchen.' She smiled at Nadine. 'Let Luc paint you, won't you? It will be a masterpiece.'

Luc laughed. 'My fan club!' he said with every sign of satisfaction. 'But it's mutual. She loves my work, and I love hers. In fact, I married her for her cooking.'

Clarrie grinned at him. 'You think he's joking, but he isn't!'

'What's for dinner tonight?' Sean asked, strolling forward, dark and romantic in the white evening jacket but his brooding blue eyes like danger signals.

'Oh, hello, Sean,' Clarrie said, lighting up with pleasure at the sight of him as women always did. 'You look very sexy!'

'Hey! Watch it, woman!' said Luc, laughing. 'Go to your kitchen immediately!'

Clarrie giggled. 'After I've told Sean what's for dinner! I'm cooking some very good grilled fish tonight, especially for Nadine, I know she likes plain fish, but this isn't really plain, it's full of flavour—it's been marinated in citrus fruit, and I'm serving it with fried banana and lime. There's also curried goat, and onion tart...I like to offer plenty of choice for every palate, but personally I'd eat the goat if I were you, Sean. It's a young goat, and the curry's very mild, I used lime and coconut milk to flavour the sauce; you'll love it.'

Nadine watched Sean smiling at Clarrie and her heart ached. He had such charm when he chose to exert it, and Clarrie was right. In that white jacket with the red silk across his waist he looked so sexy that her mouth went dry every time she saw him.

Clarrie hurried away and Luc said, 'Now, what can I get you to drink, Sean?'

Sean said he would try one of the hotel's cocktails made with coconut milk. Luc went off to get it for him and Nadine sat down at the table where her own drink waited—a tall, frosted glass of lime juice and fizzy mineral water. Sean sat down opposite, stretching his long, slim white-clad legs.

'Is that how it feels to be you, Nadine?' he drawled, and she looked at him in bewilderment.

'What are you talking about?'

'I overheard what Luc was saying about you always being reflected in mirrors and men's eyes—it sounded claustrophobic to me and you looked haunted as he said it. Is that how it feels?'

'Sometimes,' she said and his brows snapped together, a heavy black band above those brooding eyes.

'Then why do you keep modelling?' His voice was harsh, angry, and she shrank back in her seat. 'And now this TV idea! Why do you court men's attention by putting yourself on show like that unless you enjoy having them stare at you and want you!'

'I d...d...don't...it isn't like that...' she stammered, getting angry herself. 'You know how I got into modelling. It wasn't my idea; I always wanted to be an actress. I just happened to meet Jamie Colbert, and he gave me work as a model, and it seemed a good way of making money while I hoped to break into the theatre, or films...' Her voice trailed away and Sean gave her a cold, sardonic smile.

'With my help!'

She couldn't deny that she had wanted him to help her get a part in a film so she said nothing, her eyes lowered to her drink.

'Luc left that out when he was talking about men always watching you, didn't he?' Sean grated. 'He didn't mention the fact that you use men to get what you want. You used Colbert and you used me, and when I'd failed to get you what you wanted, a career in films, you left me!'

'That's not true!'

'Oh, yes, it is,' he snarled, his face hard and bitter. 'And now that Colbert's usefulness is over you'll drop him, too, won't you? Once your TV career begins you'll never see Colbert again.'

'Jamie is a friend,' she whispered, conscious of Luc coming towards them with several other members of the art class. 'And shut up. Here comes Luc with your drink.'

The next minute Luc put a cocktail in front of Sean; the glass decorated with a paper umbrella, a vivid white and scarlet orchid, and a medley of chopped tropical fruit.

'Too pretty to eat!' Sean said, pretending amusement, and one of the women from the art class sat down next to him on a bar-stool, flicked her lashes sideways at him and purred,

'Let me help you out with it!' She took the umbrella out, laughingly twirled it, then took the fleshy, gaudily coloured orchid and thrust it into her hair, before deftly picking out a piece of mango from the drink. That she slowly inserted into her kiss-shaped mouth in a sensual, deliberate fashion, while her eyes gazed invitingly at Sean, who had watched the entire performance with lazy-eyed amusement.

Nadine felt the usual sting of jealousy. It was like indigestion: a burning sensation in her chest, a bitterness in her mouth. She hated seeing him with other women.

'I'm going to paint a portrait of Nadine,' Luc announced. 'It won't be part of the coursework—you can all watch me work and see how I do it, if you like; and you can ask questions and make comments, but I'll be working with her in the afternoons so you'll still get your usual lessons.'

Nadine met Sean's hard, glittering glance; he didn't like the idea of Luc painting her, she noted with a sort of angry satisfaction. Well, she was going to do it. While Luc was painting her Sean couldn't get her alone; she would be safe from him all day, and at night she would make very sure her door was locked, until Friday, when that plane arrived to take her off the island, and that was what she wanted, wasn't it? To avoid Sean until she could get away, and once she had escaped to make sure she never saw him again.

CHAPTER SIX

GREG ERROLL rang Nadine back next morning, early, to tell her he had made all the arrangements for her trip to Miami. 'The plane will arrive at ten in the morning, so please make sure you're there, waiting for it, because they can't hang around long,' he told her, and she promised to be there punctually.

The sessions in the studio began next day in the afternoon. Right from the start there was a silent, fascinated audience who drifted in and out, watching Luc work. Their presence didn't seem to bother him and Nadine was used to being watched while she modelled, but she preferred it when, getting bored, most of the people drifted away. The atmosphere in the studio was more peaceful when there was just her and Luc.

She had no problem keeping still or holding the pose Luc arranged her in: on a dais, one knee on a chair whose back she held with both hands, her head turned over her shoulder to gaze at Luc.

Luc was an amusing companion: in fact he kept making her smile, and at first she said uncertainly, 'Is it OK if I smile? Only, if it isn't OK, would you please not be so funny?'

He laughed. 'I want you to smile. Why do you think I keep talking to you? I want you relaxed, at ease, to be yourself, not to sit there like a dummy with a blank expression. I'm not just painting what you look like on the surface; I want to paint the Nadine behind that face, and I can only glimpse her if you talk to me.'

She felt a quiver of alarm at that thought. 'Oh. That's . . . rather worrying. I'm not sure I like the idea of having my mind read!'

He laughed. 'I'm not able to read minds; it's more the personality I'm trying to pick up. Stop worrying about what I'm doing, tell me more about your modelling. How did you get into that?'

She told him about Jamie Colbert, avoiding her own reflection in the mirrors which had been set up around the room. They gave odd, partial, shifting reflections of her; Nadine found it disorientating at first but as the days went by she became so used to catching sight of herself in the mirrors that she hardly noticed them in the end.

She wished she could forget Sean as easily, but he made it hard to ignore him. She kept busy as much as she could: painting in the mornings, modelling for Luc in the afternoon. Whenever she went on the beach, though, Sean seemed to find her, and the other guests always left the place next to her free for him, although Nadine wished they wouldn't.

While she was having painting lessons he often played golf or tennis; his tan was deepening every day. Luc often held his painting class out of doors, in the garden, on the beach, but the sun was not as hot in the mornings, and Nadine wore a large straw hat. During the hottest time of the day she was always in the studio modelling for Luc, while Sean swam or sunbathed.

Sometimes he wandered into the studio, and Nadine always felt her nerves jump at the sight of him.

One afternoon when she did that Luc frowned and stopped painting. 'You've tightened up! What's wrong? Are you getting tired? Do you need a break?' He looked at his easel again, chewed on his lower lip. 'Well, I think that's enough for today, anyway. We'll stop now.'

Nadine straightened, felt pins and needles in the leg which had been propped up on the chair, and in her shoulders. She shook her arms, moving her shoulder-blades to loosen up, flexing the tired muscles.

'You need a little massage,' Luc said, coming up behind her. 'Sit down on the chair for a minute, I'll see what I can do.'

She sat obediently before she thought about it, and Luc stood behind her and began firmly massaging her shoulders, his hands deft and soothing.

She sighed with pleasure as her tense muscles relaxed. 'Oh, that's so...'

'Good?' Luc said, laughing as he let go of her. 'Feel better now?'

'I feel wonderful,' Nadine said, purring like a cat fed on cream, then Sean moved back into her line of vision, his face like thunder, blue eyes glittering and dangerous, jawline hard, mouth reined in and white with temper. Nadine's tension came back with a vengeance. She was grateful that Luc wasn't touching her any more and couldn't feel the way her muscles had knotted up again.

'Well, thank you, Luc, now I think I'll go and have a shower and rest before dinner,' she said, walking away.

Sean followed her. Nadine waited until she had almost reached her room, then, when she was sure nobody else was around she turned on him.

'Leave me alone, Sean! I'm tired and I've had enough, I can't take any more.'

'This is the first time I've seen you alone today,' he retorted angrily. 'You made sure of that, didn't you? Don't think I haven't noticed how you make sure you're surrounded by people all day so that I can't get near you; and don't pretend it's a coincidence, we both know it isn't. It's quite deliberate.'

Her chin lifted defiantly, and she shrugged. 'I wasn't going to deny it! I don't want to see you alone if I can help it.'

He was watching her intently, his blue eyes like the gleam of Caribbean waters. 'Scared, darling?' His voice had changed suddenly, become husky, intimate. It sent a shiver of sensual awareness down Nadine's spine and she swallowed.

'Scared of what?' she managed without her voice cracking, and Sean smiled at her; a crooked, mocking smile.

'Having an affair with me.'

Her colour became a wild rose, she felt the heat in her face and was furious with herself.

'No,' she burst out, and the mockery in his face grew.

'No, you aren't scared of having one? Or no, you won't have one?'

She found it very hard to think clearly while he stood so close, his blue eyes wandering over her in that disturbing fashion.

'Both!' she muttered, and his eyebrows rose.

'Both? No to both? You aren't scared of having one, but you won't have an affair all the same? That doesn't quite add up, does it, darling?'

'Stop calling me darling!'

'You always used to like it,' he said; he put a long, brown finger on her cheek and ran it very, very slowly down her throat, sending fierce tremors through her.

'And don't touch me!' She pushed his hand away and saw his eyes flash.

'You didn't say that to Luc Haines when he was fondling you just now, did you?'

The shock of his tone was like having a bucket of cold water flung over her. She jumped violently. Her nerves were as tight as a bow-string, her body rigid with tension, eyes dilated and enormous. She had known he was angry over Luc massaging her shoulders—that was one reason why she had just picked a row with him. She had been attacking before she was attacked, hoping to defuse the situation, distract him into thinking about something else.

When she recovered her powers of speech she protested shakily, 'He was massaging my shoulders! Not fondling me!'

'Whatever you call it, he was enjoying doing it to you, and you were practically purring!' Sean said with acid distaste. His eyes were cold to the point of cruelty and Nadine shivered.

'I was tired and my muscles were aching! Yes, I enjoyed being massaged, why shouldn't I? Luc has almost magic hands...'

Sean's mouth twisted. 'And you loved having them touch you!'

Her hazel eyes darkened. 'You're putting your own vile interpretation on it! There was nothing personal in what happened, nothing sexual. You're making it sound...'

'Intimate,' said Sean curtly. 'That's how it looked. Very intimate. You were leaning back against him and he was handling you as if he was used to doing so.'

Her face burned. 'Well, he isn't! Luc is a happily married man, he and I are just...'

'Don't say "good friends", please! Spare me the old, old clichés!' Sean snapped.

'Why not? It's the truth! I like Luc, he's a nice man, but I'm not interested in him sexually, any more than I'm interested in Jamie Colbert. I don't want to go to bed with either of them.'

Sean stood very still, watching her intently. 'Don't you?'

'I just told you I didn't, and I meant it!' she said, staring back angrily, her chin up.

There was a brief silence, then Sean said softly, 'What about me, Nadine? Do you want to go to bed with me?'

The low huskiness of his voice made her catch her breath, her pulses beating like jungle drums. He had caught her by surprise with that sudden change of mood and her hazel eyes filled with unguarded passion. She had to look away, look down, to hide it, her face burning; and she heard Sean's intake of breath.

He put a hand around her throat, his fingertips caressing. She felt his hand enclose her neck and was afraid he would pick up the drum of her pulses, but a moment later he put pressure on the back of her neck to force her towards him in a sudden, possessive movement, his fingers winding themselves into her long, rich chestnut hair to hold her captive and stop her struggling free.

Alarmed, she broke out hoarsely, 'No! Sean...no...'

Then his mouth came down and silenced her, his kiss hot and demanding, and Nadine began to shake. She couldn't keep her eyes open. She had entirely lost control; she wanted him so badly she was past caring about all the sensible reasons she had for not letting him back into her life. Her mouth began moving hungrily in response she couldn't hold back, her body yielding and pliant as his arm went around it and pulled her hard against him, the softness of her breasts crushed against his chest, his hard-muscled thighs pushing into her.

When Sean finally broke off the kiss it was like waking from a deep, dark dream. She groaned in protest, leaning on him because her legs were trembling, she felt weak, as if she had some strange tropical illness. Her lids fluttered back; she was blinded by the light, for a second she could barely see him, then she met those brooding blue eyes and her heart turned over.

He was looking down at her, his face tense, darkly flushed, his mouth a little apart, his breathing thickened.

'Come to bed, darling,' he whispered, and Nadine almost couldn't breathe.

She wanted to go to bed with him so much that it hurt. Dry-mouthed, she tried to say yes; her lips moved, silently, and Sean watched them with fixed attention.

'Say it, darling,' he muttered. 'Say yes.'

Nadine took a deep, painful breath, wanting to say yes, but knowing she mustn't. Slowly she shook her head.

She saw him whiten, the colour draining out of his face and leaving his eyes seeming almost black with a mixture of emotion: pain, disbelief, shock, rage.

'You want me!' he threw at her, and she couldn't deny it.

'I can't risk it again, Sean,' she whispered, tears in her eyes. 'I got hurt so much last time. We're a disaster together. Whether you call it an affair or marriage, it's still you and me, us together—and that spells disaster.'

His arms had dropped away. He was watching her, white-faced, tense, his eyes like a black hole in space, deep, cavernous, empty.

'I'm sorry,' Nadine said, and walked past him to her room. This time he didn't try to stop her. She unlocked her door and went in, shut the door behind her and bolted it, walked shakily to her bed and fell on it as if poleaxed.

She lay on her face, sobbing silently into the cover, her whole body shuddering, for minutes on end. She had had to say no to him, but it had cost her more than Sean would ever guess.

It was half an hour before she could force herself back to her feet. Walking unsteadily she went into the bathroom, showered crisply, towelled herself dry, and put on a thigh-length yellow towelling robe. She went back into the bedroom and sat down on the bed again to paint her toe-nails coral-pink. The room-maid had raised the blind, and drawn lace curtains across the open French windows. The curtains had begun to quiver in a welcome breeze off the sea which had sprung up while Nadine was in the bathroom.

While her nails dried Nadine lay on her stomach, gazing through the lace curtains, half sleepy, half weary, listening to the tropical sounds of the gardens, the croak of frogs, the whisper of the lush palms, the splash of guests in the blue swimming-pool, the clink of glasses at the pool-side bar, laughter and voices, and at a distance the soft murmur of the Caribbean rolling up on the sands.

She had never been anywhere so magical, but it was a dangerous magic because it was seeping into her, making her weaken towards Sean, when she needed to be strong.

She drifted into a light sleep, woke up some time later to realise she had to get dressed for dinner. She put on a chiffon dress which had half a dozen soft layers beneath the top one which was printed with delicate pale blue and pale pink flowers on a white background. When she walked the short skirts flared and floated around her bare tanned legs, and she had put high-heeled white strap sandals on her bare feet.

Sean was already at the table and the only empty place was next to him. She paused, hesitating; her skin prickling at the way he watched her. There was a hard, implacable edge to his face tonight: he made her very nervous.

While she dithered, he stood up and drew back her chair, gestured peremptorily. Everyone was watching them; she had no choice. She slid into the chair reluctantly, and felt his hands brush her back as he pushed her chair towards the table again before he sat down again.

'Good evening,' she said politely, glancing around the table at the other guests.

'Last one down again, Nadine,' said Karen, one of the other women from the art class, a sharp-tongued blonde in an off-the-shoulder silver-spangled dress which glittered every time she moved.

'Yes, sorry, I must have gone to sleep after my shower,' Nadine said, picking up the menu.

'That's such a beautiful dress,' one of the men from the art class said. 'So feminine and romantic.'

'Thank you,' Nadine said, smiling at him. Johnny Crewe was an accountant, he had confessed: a very ordinary man in his thirties, with hair beginning to recede slightly, pale blue eyes, and a job he found dull but which paid too well for him to risk giving it up. He was on the art course because he yearned for romance, excitement, a very different way of life. Under her smile he turned rather pink and Nadine felt Sean stiffen beside her.

'Have you chosen your meal yet?' he asked tersely, clicking his finger and thumb to summon a hovering waiter.

Nadine looked at the food on Sean's plate. 'What's that you're eating?'

'Sweet potato pancake,' he said. 'It's very good.' He forked a piece up and offered it to her. 'Try it.'

She was reluctant to; Sean pushed the fork between her closed lips. 'You'll like it.' It was almost an order. You *will* like it! he was telling her, and somehow making a public statement of ownership, telling the other men at the table that she belonged to him and ate what he told her to!

Flushing crossly, she would have liked to spit the food back out again, but he was watching her through half-closed lids, a glimmer of threat in his eyes, and eventually she ate the piece of pancake. She could not face a public scene.

'Nice, but too fattening,' she said after swallowing it. 'I think I'll have melon, and then I'll have a swordfish steak and salad.'

The waiter smilingly went off to get her first course, and Karen leaned across the table towards her, eyes enviously flicking over Nadine's dress. 'I suppose models get their clothes free?'

'Not very often, but we can usually get them at cost price if we've worn them on a shoot,' Nadine said coolly.

Johnny Crewe asked Sean, 'When are you going to put your beautiful wife in one of your films?'

'When hell freezes over,' Nadine said, and wasn't being funny.

Sean shot her a veiled glance. 'Nadine can't act, I'm afraid,' he drawled. 'But as you probably all know by now she's about to launch a new career in television, as a chat show hostess.'

Word had got out; nobody looked amazed. Johnny Crewe asked her an eager question, and Karen murmured spitefully, 'How did she get that job, I wonder?' implying by her tone that it had been Sean's influence that got the job for her.

The waiter returned with her melon, which was sliced thinly, arranged in a fan-shape, piled high with tropical fruits, flavoured with some liqueur or other, and topped off by one of the hotel's little paper umbrellas.

Nadine began to eat and Luc took charge of the conversation at the table by beginning a long anecdote about an eccentric painter he had been at art school with who had gone on to become famous by painting for films.

'Whenever Hollywood does a film about an artist it's Jack Hurley they get in to paint the pictures. He must have the most famous hands on celluloid, but nobody has ever heard of poor old Jack because his own work simply doesn't sell. Have you ever used him, Sean?'

'Once, yes. He painted what I wanted him to paint and it looked OK on film, but actually it was crude and garish. I've no idea what happened to it afterwards.'

'Talking about afterwards,' said Luc, 'we're having a display of limbo-dancing down on the beach after dinner for anyone who's interested!'

There was an excited murmur. 'Will we be able to have a shot at doing it?' asked Johnny Crewe. 'I've always wanted to do limbo-dancing.'

'Of course,' said Luc, looking amused.

When the meal was finished the guests all drifted down to the beach bar and sat around, drinking, at tables set out facing over the sands. The limbo-dancers were a noisy, lively bunch in white cut-off jeans fringed at the ends, and psychedelic shirts, violet, acid-green, explosive yellow and orange. They danced to their own music, played by a trio of drummers, on hammered steel drums, building up the crescendo of noise and movement with practised skill, making their audience laugh and shout out for more. One of the men was a fire-eater; the climax of his act was when he danced around the circle of faces watching him, juggling with fire, tossing his flambeau high into the air and catching it, drawing shapes in the air with fire, before finally dancing under the limbo bar eating fire at the same time. The hotel guests went wild with enthusiasm as he stood erect, bowing, afterwards.

Johnny Crewe got to his feet, clapping, then shouted out, 'Can I have a shot at limbo-dancing?'

'Come on up, man,' the leader of the dancers said.

Nadine watched, smiling wryly. Johnny was loving being the centre of attention, getting applause, his face flushed, his eyes very bright.

He was surprisingly supple and to everyone's amusement very quickly picked up the rhythm, moving his hips and swaying sensually, and was soon limbo-dancing as if born to it. The audience loved it and clapped noisily, then others went up to try, and Johnny called out to Nadine to join them.

She shook her head. 'No, thanks, I'll just watch.'

Johnny ran over, barefoot now, flushed and excited. 'Come on, Nadine,' he urged, grabbing her hand and pulling her to her feet. 'Dance with me!'

Sean was on his feet too; he moved like greased lightning, clamped his fingers around Johnny's wrist.

'She said no, chum! Are you deaf?'

'She can talk for herself, can't she?' Johnny said belligerently, and Nadine suddenly realised he was drunk. Sober he would never have challenged Sean, especially tonight. Tonight Sean had the look of a man poised for battle, his eyes glittering, his body as tense and lethal as an unsheathed sword. Nadine had the distinct impression that Johnny had merely given him the excuse he needed to do something violent.

'She did talk. She said no,' he told Johnny through his teeth and detached Johnny from her somehow.

'Now look——' began Johnny but never finished the sentence. The next second Sean took hold of both Johnny's shoulders, lifted him off the ground, his bare feet kicking, and hurled him backwards.

Johnny landed with a thud and a scattering of sand. Everyone else had stopped to watch the short fight. Some people actually clapped; others laughed. Johnny got up, staggered, covered in sand, and looked as if he was coming back for round two, but Luc rushed over there and caught hold of him, put an arm round him in a friendly hug.

'Come and show us all how to do it, Johnny!' He urged him back to the limbo-dancing and Johnny ambled with him.

Nadine turned on Sean furiously. 'You had no business doing that! He didn't mean any harm. He was only trying to be friendly.'

'I know what he was trying to do, and it wasn't friendship he was after,' Sean said bitingly.

She sensed the watching eyes, the listening ears, the fascinated curiosity of their fellow guests.

'Oh, shut up! You've got a nasty mind!' she told Sean and hoped they could all hear.

Turning on her heel, she walked away, down the beach, out of the ring of firelight, the yellow flares of naphtha. The shouts of the dancers and the bursts of laughter and applause died away behind her; she couldn't even see them any more as she followed the curve of the beach out of sight, but she knew that Sean had followed, was walking slowly some way behind her.

She heard the lapping of water around his legs as he strolled through the waves at the beach edge. He made no attempt to catch up with her, however; kept at a distance, as if shadowing her, like some detective in a thriller film, so she pretended she hadn't noticed him.

The moon swam silently through the deep blue sky, like a round silver fish, spreading shimmering silvery patterns in its wake like fish scales, fell across the Caribbean waters in swaths of white silk, turned the palm leaves in the garden to finest filigree, laid paths of silver through the trees and made the shadows seem blacker, almost sinister.

Nadine paused to stare out across the rippling waters towards the glimmering horizon and sighed. The scene was so peaceful: they could have been marooned on a desert island. It was easy to forget that just around the curve of the bay lay the hotel with its lighted windows and the noisy crowd on the beach with their faces lit by naphtha flares and the jewel-like coloured light bulbs around the beach-bar.

'Beautiful, isn't it?' Sean said from a few feet away, standing still, too, to gaze at the view. 'Look at that moon.'

Quietly Nadine said, 'Sean, you're ruining my holiday—haven't you any decent instincts? Why don't you go away and leave me alone?'

'My instincts tell me to stay,' he said, a step nearer.

'Then your instincts are wrong. Our marriage is over, finished, dead!'

'We've been through all that before,' he said impatiently. 'But I'll say it a hundred times, if I have to. Our marriage is legally over, but we're not finished. You know that as well as I do.'

She couldn't deny it, and, anyway, they were past that game of flight and pretence. There was just the truth now.

'Sex was never the problem, though, was it?' She moved and the water swirling around her feet fell away in little silvery fragments. She watched as intently as if it mattered, trying to fight down her awareness of the man standing behind her, his breathing warm on her bare shoulders. It was going to be hard enough to talk to him without her own senses nagging at her. 'We were always good in bed together,' she said without hiding her anger. 'The fighting started when we got out of bed.'

'We can always try staying in bed all the time!' Sean said, and her temper hit the roof.

'Even now you're refusing to take me seriously, you have to make stupid jokes!' She turned on him and stopped dead. His face was a shock to her. It could be a trick of the moonlight, but it seemed bone-white, strained, drawn.

'God knows I don't find this funny,' he muttered. 'I just don't know any other way of handling how I feel. Have you any idea how hard it is for me to admit my own feelings? Men aren't allowed to cry. We learn that at our mother's knee. We're taught to be brave little boys, little soldiers. Big boys don't cry when they fall over or get knocked down. They never show pain or fear. But we feel it, for God's sake! We get scared, and lonely, and if we always have to hide those feelings they hurt far more because we can never let them out, never ask for comfort, never cry out loud.'

She watched him, startled, taken aback. 'I never heard you talk like that before.'

'Maybe that's our trouble,' he said wryly. 'We've never really talked before, just made love.'

'Maybe,' she said, then sighed. 'No, that wasn't our trouble, Sean,' she contradicted. 'Our real trouble was that we were two people each trying to have everything our own way. And from all I can see, you haven't changed, or learnt anything. You still react with stupid, pointless jealousy every time another man comes near me. Poor harmless Johnny Crewe, just now; even Luc Haines, who anyone can see is happily married!'

His eyes darkened. 'I can't help being jealous. It's that damned job of yours. You're a sort of public icon—your face, your body, on show for everyone to stare at, and I hate knowing men stare at you. I know how they feel, because I feel like that, too. They want you as much as I do—no man could look at you and not want you.'

Colour crept up her face. The huskiness in his voice made her feel dizzy.

'If you'd ever really loved me, you would have trusted me!'

'I trust you; I just don't trust other men!'

'But it's me you're angry with!'

That stopped him in his tracks. He stared at her, frowning.

She nodded insistently. 'Yes, you were always angry with me; you wanted me to give up my job.'

'Yes,' he admitted then, and laughed shortly. 'And the irony of it is that now, I suppose, you'll be giving up modelling to concentrate on your TV work.'

'I'll have to, and my modelling would have stopped soon, anyway, because I'm getting too old for close photo work.'

'Too old at twenty-six!' he mocked, and she made a face.

'Well, that's the rules of the game in my business. You only have a few good years at the top, if you even get to the top! That's why I jumped at this offer to work on TV. I wasn't sure I could do it, but I was excited by the chance to try.'

'You'll probably be a huge success, and earn even more money!' he said wryly, and she gave him a quick, searching look.

'Talking about money, what have you managed to do about the money you need for your company?'

'I'm probably selling out,' he said in a flat, offhand tone.

'Sean!' Nadine turned pale, staring at him in shock. He stared over the moonlit water, his face blank, as if he was talking about someone entirely different.

'I had a very good offer from a guy I saw in Los Angeles while I was there the other day. I had hoped he would invest in us and leave the management intact but if he puts money in he wants control and I can't blame him.'

'But . . . your company . . .' she breathed, shattered by this news. 'You built it up, you and Larry and the others, and you had such high hopes, and everything seemed to go so well at first. I know how much it means to you, you can't sell it!'

'I don't really have much choice. We're in debt, we have to find a very large sum of money almost at once, and the banks won't lend us any more. I've been running around all our usual sources, but money is tight everywhere. Frankly, I either let the company crash, and have the vultures move in to pick the bones bare—or I sell out to someone now while I can. At least this way I get the choice of which vulture gets the company!' His voice was dry, his grimace sardonic.

'No, you mustn't sell,' Nadine burst out. She could see the depression in his blue eyes now, the pain and frustration, the sense of despair. She could see it—and she couldn't bear it. 'Larry was right, then. You must have the money back, the money you paid for my shares in the company.'

His face set hard; she saw the veins in his neck stand out as his jaw clenched. 'No!' he said harshly.

'Don't be stupid!' She was angry with him for keeping this to himself all this time. 'You've already wasted several days—I could have arranged to pay you back the money a week ago, if I'd known how desperate matters were! When Larry told me, I didn't really believe him, I thought he was exaggerating. If you'd told me all this long ago you could have saved yourself a lot of anxiety and hassle.'

'I don't want your money!' His face was pale and obstinate and she eyed him wanting to smack him.

'It isn't mine, anyway. It's yours! I never believed I had a right to that money in the first place. My solicitor kept insisting it was fair, but I didn't want it, Sean. You must have it back. It's invested safely; I'll start proceedings tomorrow to sell the shares.'

'I'm not taking money from you!' he snarled. 'I have some self-respect!'

'You're being pigheaded, Sean! Look at it as an investment, if you like—I'll lend you the money, how about that?'

He turned on his heel, walked along the beach, just as the moon slid out of sight behind a far-off little cloud, plunging the night sky into darkness, extinguishing the glitter of the waves, the silvery patina on the palms.

Nadine watched him, frowning. In this sudden darkness he looked taller, rather menacing, disturbingly male.

He spun round and came back, halted in front of her, looked down into her uplifted, watchful eyes.

'I'll take the money on one condition—you come with it.'

She stiffened. 'If you mean will I try again . . . ?' She stopped, shook her head. 'It wouldn't work, there's no point in trying.'

'It would work,' he said softly, and his fingertips slid down her bare arm and sent a shudder rippling through her whole body. Sean smiled as he saw the look on her face. He knew she wanted him; they had no secrets from each other in that sensual world they shared.

In a sudden, desperate panic she began to run, her bare feet splashing through the cool, lapping water, along the empty, whispering beach, just as the moon came out from behind the cloud and washed the coastline in silver again, sending her elongated black shadow running ahead of her.

It was a minute before she realised that she was running the wrong way. In her hurry to get away she hadn't thought about where she was going. She had just begun to run. She should have run back towards the beach party, towards the hotel grounds, and she was going in entirely the wrong direction. But by then it was too late to turn and run back. Sean was right behind her, and a few seconds later he sprang forward and caught hold of her, their bodies colliding in a sort of rugby tackle which knocked her off her feet.

She gave a choked cry, struggling. Sean fell with her, holding her, his body going into a complicated twist just before they hit the sand so that she landed on top of him, the fall softened for her by his body.

She lay there winded for an instant; then before she was over the shock Sean took her shoulders and slid her off him sideways. She found herself on her back, staring up at the milky moonlit sky.

Sean arched over her, blotting out the moon with the dark circle of his head, and she looked wildly up at him as the weight of his muscled body fell on her, splaying her against the sand.

'Don't!' she cried out.

His eyes glittered; she heard his thick breathing and felt the panic quicken in her throat.

'No, Sean! Stop it, I don't want to...'

'But that's not true, is it, Nadine?' he said gently. 'You do want me to...you're just scared of admitting it!'

She wished she could deny it but she couldn't, and it was getting worse, this aching need, because the pressure of his warm body over her, the intimacy of that urgent contact, was feeding her desire like petrol flung over a smouldering fire which would start it into flame.

'You've no right to decide what I want and what I don't,' she said, though. 'I am the only one who can say that.'

'You are saying it,' he whispered. 'Your eyes say it...' He brushed a fingertip over her lids and lashes and her eyes closed on a reflex. 'Your mouth says it,' Sean said, and lingeringly stroked her lips. 'Your whole body is saying it...'

Nadine trembled as his hand moved down over her throat, her shoulders, her breasts. 'Don't.' The brush of his flesh against her own made her blood run hotter, made her nerves leap and shiver.

'I've missed you so much,' he suddenly said, and the roughness of his voice made her pulses skip. 'I love you.'

She lay still, tears pricking at her eyes. 'Oh, Sean...'

His head came down, his mouth closing over hers in a hot compulsion that by then she was beyond resisting. Love overwhelmed her. She moaned under that mouth, under the tantalising frustration of his moving hands; her breasts ached where he touched them; her bones grew pliant, as soft as wax, and she knew that if she had tried to stand now she would have fallen down.

She had her eyes shut and was locked in a deep, devouring darkness; filled with the wind of a desire which was carrying her away like straw, like paper, in spite of herself. She loved him.

If it was going to hurt she accepted it; she couldn't deny him or herself any more just at that moment, she was past caring about anything but the satisfaction of their passion.

The fragile chiffon of her dress tore as Sean unzipped the back of it; she heard him groan impatiently. Then he was pulling it off her shoulders, dragging it downwards, and a tiny part of her mind thought ruefully of the state it would be in tomorrow, that very expensive dress which had looked so immaculate an hour ago. Now it would be covered in sand, torn, crumpled.

But that didn't matter. Sean's head was at her breast; he was kissing her pale body and breathing as if he was drowning. 'Oh, darling, darling... I need you...'

She stroked his tousled black head, caressed the nape of his neck, ran her hands down his lean back. Her eyes were shut; she didn't need to see, just felt; and once given up to her emotion she only knew she loved him and he needed her; she felt his need in every touch, every movement, every sound he made, and happiness blazed through her.

Out here on the sands with the whisper of the sea in their ears they were more alone than they had ever been before. His fame, his success, couldn't come between them, and neither could hers. They were just a man and a woman on the beach making love; the moon slid sensuously over his tanned flesh, the muscled power of his bare back, and over her white breasts with their darker aureoles around the nipples, her golden-skinned arms clasping the man to her, her loose hair.

His hands stroked along her bare thighs and she groaned, arching to meet him as he took her.

'It's been so long,' he said hoarsely. 'So long, darling, I need this badly.'

She needed it, too; she was gasping with unbelievable pleasure as the heated driving of his body moved in her; she held him, her arms tight around him, her body riding under him, her knees gripping in shudders of mounting passion.

'Sean... oh, yes... yes...' she moaned, her face taut and clenched in the rictus of desire.

She was so hot by then that she felt as though a white-hot flame was consuming her, consuming them both, and then the frenzy broke and she cried out wildly, shuddering underneath him.

Sean came too, his body convulsive, groaning harshly, as if in agony, his face hard against hers, the tension of his darkly flushed skin burning into her.

Nadine held him, cradled on her, as he almost sobbed that last descending fall of passion, and then they both lay still, dragging air into their tortured lungs, trembling as if they had run a mile.

CHAPTER SEVEN

SOMETHING whispered softly behind Nadine's head; she felt her long hair drifting away, felt something splash on her foot, and suddenly realised that the tide was coming in around them, the water cool on their overheated bodies.

A smile curved her lips. How romantic, she thought. They could lie there in the rising tide, at total peace, while the waves gently lapped over their naked bodies. How high would the tide come? She slid a look down sideways to check on the height it had reached, and saw something out of the corner of her eye. For a second she didn't realise what it was. Then, 'Oh, no!' she gasped, shocked out of her romantic haze by more down-to-earth considerations. 'My dress!'

She turned her head hurriedly, grimacing as her wet hair came up out of the water and dripped down her back. A second look told her she hadn't imagined it. She was just in time to see her chiffon dress floating away.

'Oh, no, it is...' she moaned.

'What's the matter?' Sean lazily asked, reluctant to move.

'Oh, get up,' she said, giving an angry push to the bare, broad shoulders above her.

Sean fell off with a splash. 'What did you do that for?' he asked, aggrieved.

Nadine had already scrambled to her feet and didn't bother to answer. She had more important things on her mind.

The pale chiffon dress was already bobbing over the waves some feet away from shore. Nadine waded out to get it and was soon breast-high in the water, but just as she reached for the dress a big wave came along and lifted it up, took it further away.

'Hell's bells!' she wailed, and heard Sean start to laugh behind her. He was standing on the beach, watching. Crossly Nadine looked round at him. 'Why don't you . . . ?' she began, then had to shut her mouth as the water lapped at her chin. Gurgling, she realised that she was almost out of her depth. To get her dress now she would have to swim.

She launched herself forward and swam a few ungainly strokes and at last managed to catch the trailing skirt and pull it in tow after her as she swam back to shore.

She waded out, holding the dress at arm's length. It was saturated; she looked at it and could have wept.

'I can't put this back on! How on earth am I going to get back to my room now?' She heard a smothered sound and glared at Sean. 'Oh, you think it's funny, do you?'

He grinned at her. 'If it had happened to someone else you'd laugh, wouldn't you?'

'No!' she lied. 'And, anyway, it hasn't happened to someone else, it has happened to me, and all because of you! Well, you got me into this—you can get me out! You can give me your clothes!'

'Don't be ridiculous!'

'I'm not putting this wet rag back on, and I'm not walking back into the hotel naked!'

Sean looked round. 'I could lend you my shirt...' Then he stopped talking, turned round to each side. 'Where *are* my clothes?'

Nadine looked around too. There was no sign of his short-sleeved shirt, his white jeans, all the things which he had pulled off in a hurry earlier and flung to one side.

Sean swore. He was staring out over the rolling waves. Nadine followed his stare and saw something white, identified it as his jeans; as she stared it was engulfed in another wave and vanished. Nadine began to laugh wildly.

'This isn't funny!' Sean snapped at her which made her laugh louder.

'If... if...' she stammered through her laughter, 'If this was h... happening to someone else you'd laugh!'

Sean glared for a second, then gave a reluctant grin. But it didn't last long.

'Well, funny or not, how are we going to get back into the hotel?' he demanded. 'I'm not keen on the idea of walking through that lobby like this!'

Neither was Nadine. She bit on her lip, her brow furrowed, trying to think.

For security reasons she always closed her balcony windows before she left her room, and no doubt Sean did, too, as the hotel advised. They couldn't get back in to the hotel any other way; they would have to go through the hotel lobby.

She grimly took her chiffon dress and wrung it out. 'There's no real option,' she muttered, shaking it so that water sprayed in all directions. 'I'll have to put this on!'

'Hey, you're giving me a cold shower!' complained Sean, then suggested, 'If you hang it up for half an hour it might dry off a little!'

She shook her head. 'I don't want to wait half an hour, and I'm wet myself, anyway, so what does it really matter?'

She gingerly put the dress on; not a pleasant task. She had to smooth the wet crumpled layers down over her wet body, and they felt horribly clammy on her skin. She shivered.

Sean gave her an anxious look. 'Are you OK?'

'I feel like a fish, but otherwise I'll survive,' she said drily, relieved to be covered again. She had felt very uneasy not having any clothes on at all. At any minute someone might have wandered down this end of the beach and seen them. 'I'd better get to my room quickly and get out of this dress,' she thought aloud.

As she turned to go Sean caught her arm, the contact reminding her forcibly that although she might now wear clothes Sean didn't; he was still stark naked and that made her very aware of him, very edgy. She lowered her eyes to avoid seeing that powerful body.

'Hey! What about me?' he demanded. 'You've got to get me back into the hotel. I'll lurk in the trees until I see you open your balcony windows, then I'll...' He stopped dead and groaned, then began looking around on the sand in a hurried, agitated way.

'What now?' Nadine nervously asked.

'The key to my room is in the pocket of my jeans!'

She couldn't help laughing again. 'You're kidding!'

'Do I sound as if I am?' he asked through clenched teeth, and she had to admit he didn't.

'Well, now what do we do?' said Nadine helplessly.

Sean thought, scowling. 'They'll have a spare at the reception desk; you'll have to ask them for that when you get your own key.'

'I'm not asking them for a spare key to your room!' she refused flatly. 'They'd be bound to ask awkward questions, such as, "Where is he? What do you want the key for?" And then I'd have to explain that you weren't in the hotel but I wanted to get into your room...can you imagine what they'd think?'

He looked furious. 'All right then, I'll have to sleep in your room tonight!'

The passion had dissolved; they were angry with each other again. Nadine gave him a cold glare.

'Think again! You aren't moving in with me!'

He glared back. 'What do you want me to do? Spend the night on the beach, stark naked?'

'It would serve you right if you did!'

'Thanks!' he said, seething.

'Well, this is all your fault!' she muttered.

Sean's blue eyes narrowed and flashed at her. 'It takes two, you know!'

'Not when one of them simply won't take no for an answer!' she retorted, and saw the mounting rage in his face with sudden alarm. She wasn't feeling up to one of these confrontations with him. Not that she didn't believe this was all Sean's fault, but she simply couldn't face another bitter row.

She was very cold now, the clammy material of her dress moulded to her wet body making her shiver all the time. She was constantly aware of Sean too, naked and much too close, reminding her all the time of their lovemaking a few minutes ago, when what she wanted was to forget the sweetness and agony of being in his arms.

All she wanted now was to get back to the hotel, to her room, to change into something warm and dry and then get into bed and go to sleep.

But she knew that she wouldn't be able to sleep if she knew Sean was out here on the beach all night like that.

'Look, I'll open my balcony windows and throw you out my towelling robe,' she hurriedly conceded.

'Your towelling robe?' he repeated, still glowering at her.

'Well, one towelling robe is much like another—they're sort of unisex, aren't they? You'll be able to walk back into the hotel as if you've been swimming, tell them you've lost your key, and ask for the spare one.'

'Are you blind? I'm half a foot taller than you are. I'll look ridiculous in anything of yours! Not to mention that I'm a completely different shape from you, of course! I'm not walking into the hotel dressed like something from a French farce!'

She could see he had a point. 'Well, what if you don't come in through the front of the hotel, but use my balcony? Only, if anyone sees you they may alert the hotel security people and we could find ourselves in an embarrassing situation.'

'We *are* in an embarrassing situation!' he muttered, scowling. 'It can't be much worse. You open the windows and chuck me the robe and I'll climb in through your room, and if I'm seen and the hotel security people catch me and ask questions, we'll say we were just playing at being Romeo and Juliet...'

He laughed at his own joke. Nadine didn't.

'I can imagine their faces!' was all she said.

'Who cares what they think?' Sean said with an arrogant shrug of those broad, muscled shoulders.

She looked away, biting her lip. She had already lost her head over him once tonight; she was never doing it again. If only he weren't so sexy. Look at those long, tanned legs... No, she thought, don't look at those long, tanned legs!

'Are you listening?' he asked impatiently and she nodded. He gave her flushed face a suspicious look, but said, 'OK, then once I'm in your room I'll ring the desk clerk and ask them to come up and open the connecting door between your room and mine.'

She did not want that door open, but she decided to argue about that later, when she was safely in her room and dry and warm again.

'All right,' she said, and hurried away.

The walk back to the hotel was an ordeal. At first the beach was empty, then she ran into a little group of people wandering along by the sea, talking. They stopped talking to stare at her. The two girls in the party giggled. The men mostly grinned.

'You're all wet!' one said.

'Been for a swim in your dress?' asked one of the girls.

Nadine laughed merrily. 'I had a little accident. Fell in the pool. Well, see you later!' She ran on and heard them all laughing and talking behind her. That had given them something to gossip about! She would have breakfast on her balcony tomorrow; she couldn't face the stares over the breakfast table.

She ran through the hotel gardens, avoiding any guests she saw after that, but felt people watching her and raising their eyebrows at the state she was in, and when she hurried into the hotel lobby she found Luc Haines and his wife talking to the reception clerk. Their conversation broke off, they turned to stare in disbelief at Nadine.

'What on earth happened to you?' asked Luc, skating a glance from her dishevelled wet hair down over her dishevelled wet dress to her bare, wet feet.

He was looking amused, but Clarrie's face was anxious. 'Are you OK, Nadine?'

Nadine picked up on Clarrie's tone and realised she was afraid something serious had happened to her, so she managed a weak little smile.

'Oh, I was just larking around by the pool and fell in...'

Luc roared with laughter. 'Happens all the time,' he assured her. 'You look like a bedraggled mermaid...'

Clarrie looked relieved. 'Oh, what a pity, your lovely dress!' she said sympathetically.

'I'm afraid it's ruined,' Nadine said, but Clarrie shook her head eagerly.

'No, no, we can soon get it cleaned. Put it out tomorrow morning and we'll have it looking as good as new for you by tomorrow night.'

'Thanks,' Nadine said, wondering how to explain the tear in the back, where Sean had ripped the dress off her. Flushed, she turned to ask the desk clerk for her key.

'Where's Sean?' Luc asked as the man handed it to her. 'It wasn't him who threw you in the pool, was it?'

Nadine pretended to laugh. 'Not exactly, but I blame him all the same.'

'Why do men always get the blame?' Luc asked ruefully.

'It's usually their fault!' his wife told him. 'And stop chatting to this poor girl so that she can get to her room and change out of her wet clothes!'

Nadine gave her a grateful smile. 'Goodnight, see you tomorrow!'

A minute later she was safely in her room, and as soon as the door was shut she stripped off the wet dress and put on a warm white sweater and a pair of jeans. She was about to get her own towelling robe when she remembered that the hotel provided them in the bathroom.

When she hurried in there she saw two of them on hangers behind the door. One was much larger than the other. It was intended for a man, Nadine realised, reaching for it.

She opened her french windows and walked out on to her balcony, stood there looking into the moonlit gardens, and saw Sean after a minute, a pale blur half-hidden by a palm tree. He waved his hand to tell her he was waiting, and Nadine hurled the white robe as far as she could throw it.

Sean darted forward, a running silvery streak, his bare flesh dappled by moonlight. As he came out of the shadows Nadine heard voices, footsteps. Several other guests were strolling out of the gardens towards the hotel.

Sean heard them too. She saw him slide a look sideways, then leap forward, grab up the robe, but not before the newcomers had seen him and stopped talking, indeed stopped in their tracks, their eyes wide and their mouths open.

Sean shouldered into the robe, pretending not to have seen his audience.

Shaking with laughter, Nadine leant on the balcony-rail. Sean coolly walked forward, dropped to one knee and began declaiming, '"What light through yonder window breaks? It is the east and Juliet is the sun! Arise, fair sun, and kill the envious moon..."'

Their audience laughed and began to clap. Sean got to his feet and turned to bow. 'Thank you.'

Nadine had had enough. She went back into her room and a moment later Sean joined her.

'I hope you're satisfied,' she hissed at him, 'now that you've made me the laughing stock of the whole hotel!'

'They loved it!' he said with every evidence of satisfaction. 'Think what they can tell their friends when they go home—a private performance of one of Shakespeare's greatest plays by one of the finest actors of his generation!'

'Oh, why so modest?' Nadine said coldly. 'Of any generation, surely!'

'Probably,' he agreed, a little muscle beside his mouth twitching as if he was about to burst out laughing any minute.

'I wonder why he gave up the stage to go into films and became a producer, not an actor?' she asked her nails, inspecting them closely.

Sean gave a long, theatrical sigh. 'All right, I confess—I wasn't really that brilliant on a stage, so I went into films. Maybe it's time I went back to the theatre—I could try directing a play now. I'm sure that my reputation in films would help get me a chance in the theatre. It would ensure publicity, for a start, and then plays don't cost the same sort of money.'

'You don't want to go back to the theatre!' she said, feeling like smacking him for being so defeatist. It was so unlike Sean: he had always been so strong and sure of himself and it disturbed Nadine to see him like this. 'You love making films!'

'Past tense, darling,' he said flippantly. 'Loved it. I can't afford it any more.'

'You will be able to when you get that million back.'

'I'm not taking it!'

Nadine fumed silently for a second, then threw back, 'You let me help when you got started, you borrowed money from me then, why can't you do that again?'

'You were my wife then!'

She gave him a wary look, biting her lip. Did he mean all this, or was he being devious again? 'Well . . . well, I'm your ex-wife now but surely you can still use my money! You and Larry have always borrowed money wherever you could . . .'

'That's different,' he shrugged.

'Why, for heaven's sake?' she demanded furiously.

'Because that was strictly business; they expected very high levels of return on their money.'

'You can pay me interest if that's what's bothering you!'

'No, Nadine. I'm not treating you like some city financier. It could never be business between us—it would always be personal. As I said before, I'll only take that money from you if you come with it.'

'Well, don't take it, then!' she snapped. 'Get your key from Reception and get out of my room and my life!'

He gave her a level look, his brows black and jagged, turned and picked up the phone, rang down to Reception.

Nadine went into her bathroom. She felt as if she had a cold coming. Her eyes were stinging and her throat felt as if it was full of salt. She looked grimly at herself in the mirror. You are not going to cry! she told her reflection. He isn't worth it.

Her eyes looked shadowy and glistened as if with unshed tears. You could go back to him, they said to her.

Oh, shut up! she told them.

You want to, her eyes infuriatingly said.

No, I don't, Nadine denied, her mouth as tight as a trap.

Yes, you do, her eyes said, black-rimmed as if in mourning for something, for her, perhaps, or Sean, or lost love, mislaid love, shipwrecked love which had deserved a better chance.

Only a fool would love a man who can be so maddening! she told her reflection.

Her eyes darkened with passion. Fool, they said. Fool.

She crossly bent down to the vanity unit, turned on the tap and splashed cold water on them. As she straightened, reaching for a towel to dry her face with, she heard voices in her room.

Sean's key had arrived with the desk clerk. She heard the two men laughing. No doubt Sean had made a good story out of losing his key. She hoped it didn't involve her in some way.

She waited until she heard the door close behind the desk clerk then went out, braced for another encounter with Sean, but he had gone. She looked round her room blankly and suddenly felt depressed. She missed him when he wasn't there. She had missed him ever since the day she left him, she had never really got used to living without him, and now that she had been with him for these days at the hotel she knew, with a terrible sinking inside her, that going back to being without him would be even more painful.

He wanted her back, she thought, closing her French windows and shutting out the magical moonlit night. He must be serious, or he wouldn't refuse to take her money unless she came back to him. Maybe she should...

No! she thought, making sure the desk clerk hadn't unlocked the connecting door between their rooms; then she wrote out a breakfast card and hung it on her door before she bolted it, then went into the bathroom to take a shower. Look at his jealous attack on poor, harmless Johnny Crewe, his obvious resentment because she was beginning a new career in TV. It wouldn't work. He hadn't changed. He was still possessive, jealous, demanding, set on getting his own way.

She showered off the salt and sand which had encrusted her body while they were on the beach, shampooed her damp chestnut hair, rinsed it and wrung it out before towelling it lightly, then put on her yellow lawn nightdress, cleaned her teeth, and slid into bed.

She was so exhausted by the events of the evening that she fell asleep almost at once and slept heavily all night and was woken up by the arrival of her breakfast.

She sleepily put on a matching yellow lawn wrap and stumbled to open her door for the room-service waiter, asked him to wheel the table out on to the terrace. When he had gone she splashed water on her face to wake herself up, brushed her hair lightly, and went out on to the terrace to eat the rolls and fruit she had ordered.

The day sparkled: blue sea, blue sky, water sprinklers whirling on the smooth green turf, the sun on the jewel colours of the bougainvillaea, the fretted green leaves of the palm trees whispering in the faint morning breeze. There were bodies in the gleaming blue pool, cleaving the water with gold-tanned arms; people were already lying on the loungers in the garden, their oiled bodies relaxed on spread towels, dark glasses hiding their eyes from the intrusive sun, some with straw hats on their heads.

Nadine looked down on it all grimly. She had come here for a holiday, to relax and forget her workaday problems. She hadn't counted on meeting Sean here. Now, her mind and heart were in turmoil. She kept swinging between one mood and another, one decision and another—she didn't know what to do. The only thing she did know was that the man drove her crazy.

There was a crisp London newspaper on the table beside the coffeepot. When she had finished eating she picked it up and glanced at it without much interest. The date at the top of the front page caught her eye. Thursday... Absently she thought, They get the London papers the same day, how amazing! But how do they get it here so fast?

Then she did a double-take. This couldn't be today's paper, surely?

She went back into her room and rang down to the desk. 'What day is it today?'

The desk clerk sounded startled, then amused. 'What day? Time passes very quickly here. Friday, Mrs Carmichael. It's Friday...' He gave her the full date and Nadine blankly thanked him and put the phone down.

Friday. Friday! That was the day the plane was coming to pick her up and take her to Miami to do the TV interview.

She had forgotten all about it. Too absorbed in other things, she thought grimly. She stood there, dithering, thrown into absolute disarray. What did she have to do before she left?

Shower, dress, pack some things for the couple of days she would spend in Miami. She went into the bathroom and showered, back into the bedroom, dressed in a comfortable green cotton tunic dress with a bolero jacket you could wear over it in cooler weather.

She got down her suitcase, opened it. What should she take with her? How much would she need for a few days in Miami? She looked into the crowded wardrobe, then stared at nothing for a moment.

That was when she decided—she wasn't coming back. She would fly to London from Miami. So she had to pack everything and take it all with her. And she had better pray that she didn't run into Sean before she managed to get on that plane.

She packed hurriedly, locked the cases, feeling very thirsty after her haste, so she went out to the balcony to finish the orange juice she hadn't drunk during her breakfast.

While she was drinking it she caught sight of Sean in white shirt and shorts heading out with a set of golf-clubs towards the hotel's golf-course with several other men.

Nadine stared after them, her eyes riveted by Sean's dark head, the long, lean body moving gracefully and easily over the smooth turf. She might not see him again for a long time. She needed to fix his image on her heart. Her mouth twisted bitterly. What did she mean? His image was already indelibly printed on her heart and mind.

Sadness welled up within her.

Sean and the other men vanished out of sight and Nadine walked slowly back into her room and rang the desk clerk.

'I'm flying to Miami today for several days; would you send someone up to bring my cases down?'

The plane would be landing at ten—in half an hour. She would get someone to drive her to the private landing strip now. When Sean got back from playing golf she would be long gone.

CHAPTER EIGHT

SHE met Luc in the reception lobby as she was paying her bill. 'What's all this about you leaving?' he asked, and Nadine explained that she had to leave at once.

'Bad news?' he frowned and she shook her head.

'Work, actually.'

'The boat has already gone, I'm afraid, Nadine. You'll have to wait until tomorrow now.'

'A plane is coming to fetch me, from your landing strip.'

He looked astonished. 'So that plane is coming for you! I knew one was landing around now, but I had no idea it was for you! I suppose Sean has a private jet?'

'This isn't Sean's plane, it has been chartered, I think—it's an air taxi operating out of Miami. I'm very sorry about your class and the portrait. I've enjoyed doing both, I learnt a lot and I'll certainly enjoy painting more now that I know a bit about what I'm doing—and maybe I'll be able to get back some time soon if you need me for any more work on the portrait.'

He smiled at her. 'I think I'll be able to finish it if you send me some photographs of yourself in a similar pose.'

'I'll do that, then. Thank you for everything, Luc, I've had a lovely time here. Say goodbye to Clarrie for me, she's a wonderful cook.'

'I will. She'll be sorry to miss the chance to say goodbye to you herself, but she's marketing at the moment.' Luc frowned again, looking around. 'What about Sean? I thought I saw him going off to the golf-course. Isn't he going with you?'

'No,' she said, and was saved from having to explain any further by the arrival of the taxi which was going to take her to the landing strip.

As she took off later, soaring over the palm trees and blue gleams of water, she saw the level green golf-course and little figures moving across it. One of them was Sean. She bit her lip and ached with misery, but she knew it was wiser to look away.

What she hadn't expected was to find Jamie waiting for her when she reached Miami airport. He waved as she came through the barrier, following the porter who was pushing her luggage.

'Hi, Nadine!'

'Jamie, what on earth are you doing here!'

They hugged, kissed each other on the cheek. 'I'm on the show tonight,' he told her. 'I've got a car waiting—you'll love it, bright pink, like bubblegum, and several blocks long!'

'You're on the show?' That startled her; she stared at him, open-mouthed, and he grinned at her.

'Greg Erroll didn't tell you? Yes, the TV people here wanted us both. It made a good show because they have Cara Marquez, too... remember her? I discovered her working in a McDonald's in London when she was a student, and after I'd done some work with her she became a top model in the States. She's a Florida girl, born here in Miami, so the TV people want to link the three of us in this show.'

'It makes sense,' she agreed. She had met Cara several times and liked her. A dark, dramatic girl with Latin colouring and a fabulous figure, Cara was still only twenty-two; she would be earning top money for quite a while yet.

'We'd better hurry, I'll take you to the hotel to book in and leave your luggage, and then the TV people want time to talk to you before the show,' Jamie said, steering her towards the exit.

He was attracting attention from a party of girls who had just flown in to Miami for a beach holiday. They were staring at Jamie, whispering and giggling, but it was unlikely any of them had recognised him as a famous photographer. Jamie was just so sexy: a live-wire of a man, electrically magnetic with his black eyes and hair, and that terrific energy. He was dressed with tremendous style too—his thin, graceful body sheathed in black and white; a black shirt and white tie, white jeans, black trainers. It was hard to believe his real age; you had to look very close to see the faint lines in his heavily tanned face.

Greg had booked them both into the Grand Bay hotel in Miami's Coconut Grove, an expensive, fashionable area of the city.

'I must have time to freshen up,' insisted Nadine, and went up to her room at once to shower and change out of the clothes she had worn during her flight. Jamie headed, meanwhile, for the bar lounge. Before going down to join him Nadine stood at her window and gazed out, entranced, over the panoramic views across the bay. Biscayne Bay was a busy place: white-sailed yachts skimmed like dragonflies across the blue water, speedboats buzzed between landing stages, and across the bay she could see the homes of millionaires, mock-Tudor residences, or Spanish gabled houses, set in immaculate gardens running down to the water's edge; mostly with luxury yachts tied up at their private landing stages. Around the hotel stood an intriguing mix of expensive boutiques, high-rise apartment blocks, and much older houses built, Jamie had told her, of coral rock, a local material she had never seen before.

The phone jangled, making her start. She ran to answer it. It was Jamie.

'Nadine, can we get on our way? I promised to get you to the TV studios half an hour ago!'

'I'm coming,' she promised.

Cara Marquez was already there with the production team, drinking black coffee out of paper cups. She kissed Nadine on each cheek.

'Hi, you guys!' It was always a surprise to realise she didn't have a Spanish accent, she looked so Spanish—and was, of course, a hundred per cent Spanish by blood but second-generation American, Miami-born. Nadine often envied her—Cara had it all: beauty, charm, and brains. She had not only made a fortune with modelling since she met Jamie in London three years ago, she had actually managed to get a degree in English and French literature at the same time!

The producer's researcher led Nadine off into a little office to ask her a string of questions scribbled down on a clipboard. Outside she could see Cara and Jamie dancing together while the show's little band rehearsed their music.

The presenter arrived and was introduced, stared at Nadine, took the clipboard from the researcher and skimmed down the answers Nadine had given.

'You were married to Sean Carmichael?' Her eyes lifted, narrowed.

Nadine nodded, her face tightening in anticipation of questions about Sean. He was the last thing she wanted to talk about.

The presenter looked at the researcher. 'We should have got him too, he's in the news at the moment. His film company just bombed.'

'It has done nothing of the kind! Where did you hear that?' Nadine flared, a dark red colour coming into her face.

The presenter shrugged. 'A friend works for the company in London and she's scared for her job, she told me the other day.'

'Well, she needn't be. His company is just fine, I ought to know, I'm about to invest a very large sum of money in it. I wouldn't do that if there was any risk attached.'

'All the same, we might talk about that on the show,' said the presenter to the researcher.

'No!' Nadine said shortly.

The other two ignored her. She bit her lip and from then on was haunted by the fear that they would bring up the subject of Sean and his company on the air without warning. It could cause him terrible damage if his financial problems were talked about on American television, and although Nadine had run away from him she couldn't help feeling protective towards him. It hurt her to see Sean failing, losing face. She knew how his ego would get dented and Sean's ego was a vital part of him.

In the event, Sean was barely mentioned on the show, except in passing, when the presenter introduced her, saying that she had once been married to Sean Carmichael, the film producer. Nadine wasn't the main focus of the show at all, as it turned out. Cara was: she was the local girl and she was a very big name in Florida. Nadine's name was nowhere near as well known, so the interview with her was cut short in order to make more time for Cara and Jamie.

'I don't really know why they had me on the show at all! It was a waste of money for Greg to get me over here in an air taxi!' she said to Jamie next day at an early breakfast in the hotel.

He was eating waffles with maple syrup. Nadine was eating a bowl of fresh fruit muesli and looked at him in disbelief as, having finished his waffles, he ordered wholegrain toast and when it arrived spread it with golden butter and honey.

It was infuriating that he could eat so much without putting on an ounce, especially at that hour in the morning, when Nadine never felt hungry; but then he burnt up energy at a terrific rate.

'Oh, there's method in Greg's madness—he likes to co-operate with American TV companies, hoping they'll buy his shows one day. It may have cost him a lot of money but it's seed corn for the future.' Jamie poured himself more of the excellent coffee and added cream. 'Now, what shall we do today? I'm not going home until Monday, and Greg said you were booked in here for several days.'

She nodded. 'I want to look at the shops—Greg said they were fabulous.'

Jamie grimaced. 'Oh, shopping! How boring. Why do women love to do it? That can wait. Come sightseeing with me. I'm longing to see Key West again. I was here years ago and loved it. There is a tedious long drive across the causeway which links all the keys; you can't pass other cars and tend to drive in convoys led by the slowest car—you know what that can be like! But the scenery is breathtaking.'

'I remember a film with Humphrey Bogart in it . . . and Lauren Bacall, I think . . . I'm sure it was called *Key West*, but all I remember of it is storms lashing around a harbour.'

Jamie laughed. 'I know the film you mean. It was called *Key Largo*, I think. Key West is right at the tip of the archipelago, and it's unique, you'll love it. I've hired a car—no, not the bubblegum limo I met you with at the airport! This is a small Ford and doesn't eat petrol. We'll go right after breakfast, shall we? Meet you in the lobby in half an hour. We'll need to leave early—it's a very long drive, there and back. We'll eat lunch in Key West.'

The drive across the causeway was a long, slow one, as Jamie had warned; but while they drove Nadine was fascinated by the view on either side. Jamie had bought a guidebook and Nadine skimmed through it as they drove.

'There are forty-two islands along the Keys, and forty-two bridges linking each island into the chain. And those strange trees sticking up out of the water are mangroves...they have roots like stilts, and sort of float on the water, it says in here—aren't they weird?'

'Look at that—I'm sure it's a brown heron!' Jamie said, staring at a large brown bird nesting on a telegraph pole high above them.

Nadine screwed up her eyes in the fierce sunlight. 'I'm not a bird expert, but it does look sort of heron-like. If it would unfold its legs we could see it better.'

'Audubon, the American bird painter, lived out here for some years,' Jamie casually murmured, 'working on paintings of Florida birds. If we had time we could visit the house where he lived, in Key West.'

Nadine gave Jamie an amused look. 'Is that why you were so set on coming out here? To see Audubon's house?' She knew Jamie was a fanatic about birds and pursued glimpses of them in all the wild places of the countries he visited.

He grinned sideways at her. 'It was one reason, but Key West has a lot more to offer than that. If you like, while I'm visiting the Audubon house you could take a ride on the Conch Train.'

'On the what?'

'It's a tram, more than a train, actually, but they call it the Conch Train,' he said, laughing. 'The local people call themselves Conchs, by the way; after the conch shells, I suppose. You can buy them everywhere in Key West.'

'Don't tell me the Conch Train is shaped like a shell?'

Jamie roared. 'No, that's just the name they give it.'

Once she had seen the Conch Train she had to have a trip on it around the streets of Key West. It was more of a tram than a train, open on all sides, but with a fluttering canopy overhead, making the ride a pleasure on such a hot day, as a little breeze kept fanning Nadine's flushed cheeks.

The driver talked them round the sites of the town as they slowly navigated their ways between the extraordinary houses, most of them frame-built, of painted wood, with wooden painted gingerbread decoration along the gabled roofs, and the balustrades of terraces. The gingerbread had been carved by generations of deep-sea fishermen while they were away for months; it was brought back as a present for their wives when they returned and the wives had competed with each other: each wanting to have the most gingerbread decoration along their houses because it symbolised their husband's love for them.

Jamie and Nadine met up when she got off the Conch Train, and they decided to lunch in Old Mallory Square, choosing local dishes—a delicious chowder made with tomato and sweetcorn, very spicy and hot, locally caught fish steaks served with salad, followed by Key lime pie, which turned out to be yellow rather than green, but, the waiter assured them, was meant to be that colour.

After lunch, they visited Ernest Hemingway's house, stared at what they were assured was original furnishing, and talked about the books he had written during his time there—*To Have and Have Not*, and *For Whom the Bell Tolls*. Then they walked around tracking down the places where various other famous American writers had stayed—the town had obviously been a magnet for writers—Tennessee Williams, Dos Passos, Robert Frost, all had been drawn there at one time or another. Jamie took photos everywhere they went; he never travelled without his camera.

Before they drove back to Miami they followed the crowds of tourists on to the wooden boardwalk beside the ocean to watch the sun sink below the horizon, colouring the sea and sky with flame. Jamie took lots more photos. He had plenty of material to choose from. There was a carnival atmosphere around them: artists sold their canvases, craftspeople sold jewellery, leatherwork, hand-dyed clothes. Entertainers danced, or sang, or played instruments. There were several mime artists with the traditional white-painted faces in black suits.

Nadine felt pleasantly sleepy as they set off on the journey back to Miami. 'You were right, Key West was fascinating,' she told Jamie, who smiled.

'I'm glad you liked it. Then tomorrow you can do your shopping!'

She was so tired after all the walking they had done in Key West that she fell asleep the minute her head hit the pillow, and didn't wake up until late next day. She had breakfast with Jamie, who had come down late too, and then they separated—she went shopping, and Jamie went off with his camera to take some pictures.

Next day they both flew back to London on Concorde. The flight took half the time the usual jet took, but they still felt stiff and weary when they arrived.

As they walked through the barrier on their way out to get a taxi, Nadine suddenly saw Sean, in a white jacket, standing among the crowds thronging the barrier, waiting for arriving passengers. You couldn't miss him; his black head showed above those around him, his brooding blue eyes narrowed and angry as he looked from her to Jamie.

Her pulses skipped and she became breathless. What was he doing here? Had he come to meet her? But how would he know which plane she would be on? Maybe Greg Erroll had told him? But maybe he was meeting someone else? Or had he just arrived, himself, from the West Indies? If so, where was his luggage, though?

Her steps slowed, her mouth went dry—he looked so harsh, his mouth set in a forbidding line; she was afraid of facing him.

'What's wrong? You've gone pale; is it jet-lag?' asked Jamie, sliding an arm around her.

'I suppose so,' she muttered, moving away from him because she knew how angry it would make Sean to see Jamie holding her like that. She shot a look towards where Sean had been, and then her eyes widened. He had gone. Had he seen Jamie put an arm round her in that intimate gesture? Her heart sank.

She knew very well what he would have thought, seeing her arrive with Jamie, after leaving the hotel without warning. If Greg had explained about the TV interview, of course, Sean would realise that she and Jamie had been in Miami to do that show, but from the expression on his face he had not expected her to arrive with Jamie. No doubt he had put two and two together and come up with a totally wrong answer for the sum. He had always been suspicious of her relationship with Jamie. Nothing had changed.

On the way to the taxi rank she kept looking around for Sean but he had vanished without trace. She and Jamie shared a cab into London—he dropped her first before going on to his own home. It was a warm May day; there was white lilac in bloom in the garden at the back of her flat. She opened a window and the scent of lilac drifted in, filling the room. For no reason she could pin down, tears filled her eyes. What was she going to do about Sean?

Nadine had slept on the plane and didn't feel like going back to bed, so she began making phone calls. First, she made several business calls, and then she rang Larry Dean, at his office, and was put through at once.

He sounded startled. 'Nadine! Hello, how are you? Are you back? Did you have a good holiday? I thought you were going for several weeks.'

'I had to come back early. Larry, where's Sean?'

'Sean?' He sounded wary. 'I . . . I'm not sure . . .'

'I know he's in London, I saw him at the airport.'

'Did you?' Larry's voice became worried. 'What on earth was he doing there? He wasn't getting a flight, was he?'

She frowned. If Larry was anxious about Sean there had to be a good reason. 'I have no idea,' she said slowly. 'I thought you might know. Did he tell you he came out to the West Indies to see me?'

Larry was silent, then said uneasily, 'Yes, I knew he'd been over there. I assumed he went to ask you for money, but he said he didn't. What on earth is going on, Nadine? Can you tell me what his plans are? I don't know, he won't talk about it, and things are getting to crisis point here. I can't pay the wages this month and once that gets out we're finished.'

She bit her lower lip, frowning. 'If I lend you my million, will that save you? Or will it get eaten up in paying your debts without actually fuelling a new project? Because I don't want to throw my money into a big black hole, you know.'

Larry's voice was cautiously eager. 'Of course not, that's very understandable, I promise I wouldn't let your money get swallowed up like that—it would help us launch a new project, Nadine. If we had a sum of that size in cash in the bank we could pay off our most pressing debts first of all, but more importantly we could interest bigger investors to back Sean's new plans. Actually, we're hopeful that the mini-series has got a definite buyer.'

'Greg Erroll?' she guessed and Larry laughed.

'Well, Greg is still reluctant to get off the fence—he won't say yes or no, he keeps asking for time to make up his mind. But another buyer has come forward.'

'Who?'

'I can't talk about it yet, but by tomorrow we'll know for sure whether or not this company is going to sign a contract, and if it does we're back in business.'

'Does that mean you won't need my money?'

'No, no, we do need it, but if this guy signs the contract tomorrow then we'll be able to give you a much stronger guarantee if you do lend us the million. How easy will it be for you to have the money in cash? Will it take you time to sell investments?'

'I've already started the process. The cash should be in my bank within a week. Will that be time enough?'

Larry gave a long, rough sigh. 'Yes, fine, thanks, Nadine. I can't tell you how grateful I am, and I'll let you know as soon as Sean makes contact.'

'And let me know if this buyer for the mini-series signs the contract,' she said—because a sale at that stage would probably make Sean feel better.

Larry rang her early next morning, sounding nervous and agitated. 'Nadine, I'm sorry but...how much could you raise at once? We badly need enough cash to pay a nasty piece of work who is threatening legal action immediately if we don't pay now.'

She frowned, thinking quickly. 'Well, I think I could write out a cheque for twenty thousand pounds without it bouncing! Would that be any good?'

'It would be wonderful. I'm sorry to ask... but how soon could we have it? The nasty piece of work is here, in my office, and won't leave empty-handed.'

'I'm on my way,' Nadine said.

'I could send someone...' began Larry.

'No, I'd better come myself.'

'Thank you, Nadine,' Larry said gratefully. 'I can't tell you how much I appreciate this.'

She arrived at the film company offices half an hour later with the cheque already written out in her handbag. She was shown up into Larry's office immediately.

Larry was sitting behind his desk looking distinctly harassed and leaning against the wall was a hulking great brute in a horrible acid-green suit who wore black sunglasses on his nose and what looked to Nadine like a false moustache.

Nadine ignored him, gave Larry a soothing smile, took the cheque out of her bag and handed it over the desk to Larry who read it carefully and then gave a sigh of relief.

'Thanks, Nadine.' His look was gratitude enough, then he picked up a document from the desk. 'Right, then, sign for this, would you?' he said pushing the piece of paper across the desk in the direction of the man in the vile green suit.

The brute read the document slowly, his large finger following the lines of type, scowling over it, then said in a rough, East End accent, 'Look 'ere, I'm not signing nothing till I've made sure the cheque won't bounce. Give me the number of her bank so I can check with the manager.'

Larry looked helplessly at Nadine. Coldly she looked in her address book and gave the brute the telephone number. He rang her bank and asked to speak to the manager, then had a short conversation before handing the phone to Nadine.

'He says he wants to talk to you before he'll tell me anything about your account.'

She spoke to her bank manager, who was clearly eaten up with curiosity, reassured him that the money was a business deal and it really was her speaking, then she handed the phone back to the brute who talked to the manager again before hanging up.

'OK, now we're in business,' he said. 'Where do I sign?'

He scribbled an unreadable signature then slipped the cheque into his wallet, nodded to Larry and then as an afterthought to Nadine.

'When I provide equipment I expect to get paid for it, as agreed,' he said as if justifying himself, then left, letting the door bang behind him.

'Equipment?' Nadine asked Larry who grimaced.

'Electronic stuff, sound equipment—it costs the earth, and our head of sound said he knew this man who could supply it cheaper than our usual people.'

'Oh, Larry! How could you make such a stupid mistake? You know deals like that are always with crooks!'

Larry looked rueful. 'We were desperate. And you're right, that man is an absolute crook! He has some very vicious friends who break things if you make them angry, he says. They break people too, as a last resort, he told me. I'm very relieved to have got him out of my life. We'll never buy anything from that source again!' He came round the desk and gave Nadine a warm hug. 'Thanks, Nadine, I can't say it adequately... but thanks.'

She kissed him lightly. 'My pleasure...'

Behind them the door opened and they both felt the freezing wind of disapproval coming their way. Larry stepped back, looking alarmed. Nadine turned round, hazel eyes wide with a muddled mixture of shock and relief.

'What the hell is going on here?' Sean demanded through his teeth. 'And why was Buzz Brown looking so pleased with himself as he went just now?'

'Nadine paid him off,' Larry gabbled.

Sean hit the roof. 'She did what? You asked her for money to pay that rat off? I told you to leave her out of my business affairs! How dare you go to her behind my back again, after everything I said, and ask her for money!' He took three strides and grabbed Larry by the collar, hauling him up on to his toes and shaking him as a terrier would shake a rat it had cornered. 'I ought to break your neck!'

Larry had gone red in the face and was choking. 'Sean . . . for heaven's sake . . .'

Nadine leapt across the room at Sean, grabbed his hands and tried to break their hold on Larry.

'Let him go! Let him go, Sean! Are you mad? You're choking him to death!'

Sean hurled Larry to the other side of the office, where he fell into his own chair and slumped there looking dazed. Sean turned to Nadine, his blue eyes blazing with a menace she found infinitely more disturbing than she had found the glowers of the hulking brute who had just left.

'Larry deserved that,' Sean said grimly. 'And now it's your turn! I told you I didn't want your money, didn't I? But you never listen. You've ignored everything I said and now you're going to have to take the consequences!'

'Don't you shout at me, Sean Carmichael!' Her voice shook slightly; she hoped he wouldn't notice. She hated it when he was so angry: the male aggression made her nerves quiver with tension.

'I am not shouting,' he shouted. 'I told you I would only take money from you on one condition—don't pretend you've forgotten. Well, you've handed over a lot of money to the company, and now I'm going to insist that you fulfil the condition too. I am not——'

Larry was sitting up, straightening his collar and tie, brushing back his hair, looking puzzled. 'What condition?' he interrupted.

Sean stopped talking, his face startled, as if he had forgotten Larry was there. He swung round to eye him threateningly. 'Haven't you left yet? There's the door, get out.'

'This is my office, Sean!' protested Larry.

'I'm borrowing it.' Sean's voice was at its most arrogant. 'Get out.'

Larry got up, shuffled to the door looking uneasy but made a last effort to intervene before he went. 'Now, Sean, don't bully Nadine any more. She's done us the most enormous favour and you ought to be grateful, not bellow at her...'

'Get out!' Sean roared.

Larry gulped and vanished, banging the door behind him.

Sean turned his dangerous blue eyes on Nadine and a quiver ran through her. 'Now...as I was saying...if I take your money, you come with it.'

CHAPTER NINE

'DON'T be ridiculous!' Nadine darted towards the door but he got there first, barring her way, too tall, too powerful, for her to push him aside, so she stopped and lifted her chin defiantly. 'And don't you threaten me, Sean!'

'I'm keeping my temper,' he said, incredibly, because he was looking like a volcano about to erupt. 'But I can't promise to keep it for long, so tell me what I want to know before I get really angry. I know you left the island to do some TV show in Miami. I found out that Greg Erroll had booked the private plane that picked you up, and I rang him and Greg told me about the show, but he thought you were coming back to the island when you'd done it. So I waited for you.' His blue eyes burnt down into her like branding irons. 'But you didn't come back, did you? Instead, you spent time in Miami with Jamie Colbert—did you sleep with him?'

Very flushed, she crossly shook her head. 'I told you once, I have never slept with Jamie and I never will! I'm very fond of him and I know he's fond of me, but we're friends, not lovers.'

'Hmm.' Sean didn't sound convinced. 'But you spent several days in Miami alone with him!'

'Sightseeing. We were sightseeing! Jamie had his camera; he took endless photographs. If he has a mistress, that's it—his camera, not me! He'd hired a car, we drove around the Everglades, right down the Keys to Key West, we drove around Miami, I shopped and we swam in the hotel pool and sunbathed on the beach. We had a few peaceful days' holiday...'

'Together!' Sean made the word sound like an accusation, his face tense.

'Yes, together,' she agreed impatiently. 'Friends do go on holiday together, all the time.'

'If you wanted to continue your holiday why didn't you come back to the island?'

She laughed disbelievingly. 'With you there? Peaceful? Are you kidding?'

His face tightened as if she had hit him. 'So you admit it—you didn't come back to the island to avoid me!'

She didn't answer that, her lashes lowered over her eyes, her hands restless.

Sean waited, then said harshly, 'You stayed on in Miami alone with him, and then you flew back with him to London. I might be sitting in the West Indies now, waiting for you, if I hadn't got tired of waiting and rung your hotel. You weren't in, but I did find out that you were due to check out next day and fly back to London. I thought the hotel might have made a mistake about your flight, so I checked up with the airport and found out that you were booked on a London flight. So I got a plane back myself, intending to meet you at Heathrow when you arrived.'

'I saw you,' Nadine muttered. 'Don't think I didn't see you lurking there! So if you'd come to meet me, why did you rush off without a word?'

His blue eyes glittered at her. 'Why do you think?'

She refused to answer on the grounds that it might incriminate her.

'Yes,' Sean said. 'Because Colbert was with you, wasn't he? Whether you say he's a friend or a lover, there he was, with his arm around you in a very possessive way—so I left.'

'Well, if you were going to talk to Jamie the way you've been talking to me I'm glad you did! He would have thought you were crazy if you'd rushed up and made angry noises at him over nothing! That's just why I left the island. I was having a wonderful time learning to paint, I liked Luc and Clarrie Haines, the food was delicious, the island a dream . . . but once you arrived I never had a minute's peace, did I? You were like a wasp at a picnic on the beach. You buzzed around all the time, making me nervous; I couldn't relax or enjoy myself. As you wouldn't leave, I decided I had to.'

He watched her, his brows very black above those bright blue eyes. 'If you hate me so much, why are you here?' he bit out, and she jumped, her face white then red.

'Hate you? I didn't say I hated you!' She saw his eyes narrow and gleam, and hurriedly went on, 'And anyway, I told you, Larry rang me and asked me to help—what was I supposed to do? Refuse point-blank?'

'Larry had no business asking you for money! I made it crystal-clear to him that I did not want him involving you!'

'How can I not be involved?' she flared. 'The company means something to me, too, you know. I've been in on it from the beginning, I don't want to see it going bankrupt if there's anything I can do to stop it.'

'But this isn't simply a question of money, is it?' Sean murmured softly, and her mouth went dry at the way he looked at her. 'The real question is...are you coming back to me or not? If you're not, you can take your money away, I don't want it.'

'I'd have to be insane to come back to a man who gets jealous over nothing, won't listen to reason, wants to control my entire life!'

He caught her face between his hands and said huskily, 'It will be different this time, Nadine! I'll try not to get jealous...'

'Oh, yes?' she asked him with a cynical smile. 'For how long? While we were on the island I kept telling you I wasn't having an affair with Jamie, I'd never had an affair with Jamie, but you still exploded because you saw me with him at the airport!'

His mouth indented. 'I said I'd try! I didn't say I'd always manage it. I can't help being jealous of you; I love you so much it makes me see red whenever another man goes near you.'

Her heart turned over and she felt her knees go weak, but she couldn't let the pattern repeat itself all over again. She had to be firm with him. 'Can't you see how embarrassing that is for me, not to mention what a strain it is to have you going into a rage if another man says hello to me?'

He frowned. 'Yes, it must be. I hadn't thought of it like that, Nadine.'

'Not to mention the fact that it means you don't trust me an inch—how do you think I feel about that?'

She felt the sigh he gave. 'I told you! I do trust you! It's them, not you, I'm afraid of.'

Nadine froze, staring up at his tense, pale face.

'Afraid of?' she repeated and saw the dark flush crawl up his face, saw his jaw tighten.

'What I meant was . . .' He broke off, groaning. 'No, that was what I meant—I've always been afraid I'd lose you. You know my parents were divorced—my mother was a very beautiful woman. She went off with another man when I was fourteen, and my father took it very badly. I watched him fall apart—it ruined his life—and I swore to myself then that I'd never let that happen to me, I'd never care that much about any woman. Then I met you and I couldn't help myself. I cared, badly, and I was terrified that some day someone would come along and take you away from me the way somebody took my mother from my father.'

She had known that his parents had divorced when he was in his teens, and that his father had died of a heart attack a few years later. She had met his mother only once or twice since the older woman was currently with her third husband in the States and had shown no real interest in either her son or his wife; but this was the first time Sean had ever told her how his parents' marriage had broken up and how it had affected him, and it altered everything.

Huskily she said, 'Why didn't you tell me all this long ago?'

'I hate talking about it!'

'But can't you see what a difference it makes, to understand why you should be the way you are? It makes sense of what seemed completely crazy.'

He watched her intently, his blue eyes dark with emotion. 'Does it? I wish I could make sense of you, darling. When we were together on the island I was so sure you loved me, every response you gave was so strong; and yet you suddenly flew off without even leaving me a note! How could you do that to me?'

'I had to get away, I was in such a muddle. You aren't the only one who has been scared, Sean. I was terrified. I'd been trying to live without you since we split up and not doing very well, but at least life was more peaceful, and then you arrived at the hotel and from then on I felt like someone on a roller-coaster ride, never knowing what would happen next, my life utterly out of control. When we made love it got worse, I got more scared—I had to get away and think.'

'And now?' he whispered. 'How do you feel now, Nadine?'

She looked at him helplessly, still torn between her aching need for him and her own common sense, and his eyes flared.

'Darling,' he said in a low, hoarse murmur, and then his mouth came down, searching for hers, and she swayed towards him like a sapling in a gale, unable to fight or resist. She should have run for the nearest exit the minute she saw him again, at the TV studios, or, if not then, when he turned up in her bed at the hotel on the island. She should have fled at the first symptom, not left it until it was too late. It was too late to escape: she admitted that as his mouth trapped hers and hungrily demanded a response, as his arms went round her and drew her so close that she could scarcely breathe. She didn't even try to escape. She moaned and ran her own arms round his neck and kissed him back with a passion as deep and hot as his.

The whole world seemed to stop spinning, they were poised together in a bewitched silence, their eyes shut, their bodies clinging, their mouths moving passionately.

Then the phone rang. They were so hyper-tense that the noise was like a gun-shot. They leapt apart, eyes flying open, dazed. Then Sean swore under his breath, turned and bellowed towards the door leading into Larry's secretary's office. 'Answer that phone, can't you, Miss Simmonds?'

There was a brief silence, then a tapping at the door.

'Well?' Sean roared. The tapping came again, and he snapped, 'Oh, come in!'

The door opened. Nadine hurriedly moved away and stood by the window looking out, breathless and very flushed, nervously straightening her dishevelled hair with one hand.

'Sorry, Mr Carmichael, but it was me ringing you,' Larry's secretary mumbled. 'Only there's an urgent call for you and Mr Dean had told me not to disturb you, but you had said if Mr Salvatore rang to put him through at once, so I didn't know what to do, so I rang you to ask...'

'Why didn't you tell me at once?' Sean bit out. 'Are you too stupid to follow instructions? Put the call through here now.'

'Yes, Mr Carmichael, of course, sorry...' The secretary sounded as if she was going to cry. She rushed out and Nadine turned to give Sean a wry glance.

'Poor girl, why do you bully her like that? She does her best.'

'Her best is not good enough,' he retorted. 'That call was urgent. I told her a dozen times to make sure it was put through at once but she still dithered.'

'She explained—Larry told her not to disturb us. It's not surprising if she was in a quandary.'

The telephone on the desk began to ring. Sean looked at it, but didn't pick it up. Instead he said to her, 'This won't take long, darling, then we'll go out for lunch.'

She nodded and sat down. Sean picked up the phone.

'Good morning to you, Sal, how are you?' He sounded energetic, very positive. 'Yes, I'm fine. How did your wife enjoy the opera last night? Oh? Well, Wagner can be very noisy if you have a headache. Jet-lag too? Yes, it is never wise to drink too much wine on a long flight. It always makes jet-lag worse. Personally, I try not to drink anything but water or fruit juice on a long flight. Tell your wife to go for a walk around the shops, eat a light lunch and then go to bed for the afternoon. That may help.' He paused, listened, laughing. 'Yes, with or without company.' Another pause, then his face lit up and he smiled broadly. 'I am very happy to hear that. Yes, I do agree. I think we will make good partners, Sal.'

Nadine stiffened. Partners? What did that mean? Was this the man who wanted to get control of Sean's company? Was he offering different terms after all?

Sean said calmly, 'I'll get my people on to drawing up the agreement immediately. Well, if you prefer a joint discussion before the agreement is drawn up...yes, certainly, we can accommodate you there. Yes, I'll be here. I'm not in my office at the moment, so I can't give you an answer on that, but I don't think I have an engagement tomorrow night. May I ring you back?'

He laughed and Nadine picked up a different note in his voice; a hint of relief, of satisfaction, even of triumph.

'Good. I'm very pleased about this, Sal. I look forward to seeing you tomorrow afternoon and later today I'll be in touch with a definite answer about dinner tomorrow. Oh, by the way, will your wife be there? I'd like to bring my wife if I may.' He listened, then said, 'Thank you, I'll tell her. And I'll get back to you soon.'

He put the phone down and did a sort of triumphal leap, punching the air as he did so.

'It worked! It worked!'

'What was all that about?' Nadine asked, watching him with a little smile. He looked like a little boy who had won a sports trophy.

He came over to her and kissed her, giving her a fierce hug. 'Our money problems are over. You remember I told you I'd had an offer for the company? Well, while I was on the island I talked to an old friend in the film business who is something of a fixer, and he casually talked to Enrico Salvatore—the TV producer, you must have heard of him, he's backed some of the biggest, glossiest productions to come out of New York in the last five years. When Sal heard I was thinking of selling out, but wasn't too happy with the terms of the deal, and wanted a partnership rather than an outright buy-out, he asked how I'd feel about a partnership with him—which was precisely what I did want, of course. He's in London at the moment, so he rang me yesterday and we talked, kicked the idea around, then got down to discussing terms, and then Sal said he had to consult his board, and would get back to me. Just now he told me the partnership had been approved, and as soon as I sign the agreement the money will be forthcoming. So our troubles are over.'

'And you won't need my money,' Nadine said wryly.

He stroked her chestnut hair with a tender hand. 'If you want to invest it in our company we'll be very happy to have it, on the same conditions.'

She looked at him in bewilderment. 'The same as Enrico Salvatore?'

'No, the same as they were before Sal rang,' he said with a mocking little smile. 'I'll take your money only if you come with it, and if you would rather keep the money invested in something less risky that's fine by me, so long as I still get you.'

She wryly shook her head. 'You made that money in the first place. I'd always have been happy to hang on to my shares; it was you who insisted on buying me out of the company.'

'Well, after the divorce I thought you were going to marry Colbert, and I didn't want him within a mile of my company. What I would have liked to do was kill the pair of you, but as I couldn't do that I settled for a stupid dramatic gesture, and insisted that you sell me back those shares. I told myself I didn't want anything more to do with you, I wanted you out of my life but the truth was I was hurting too much to know what I was doing.'

She gave him a sideways look, her lip caught between her teeth in an uncertain gesture. 'Sean...'

'Yes, darling?' he said, winnowing her chestnut hair with his long brown fingers.

'Before we make any decisions we ought to talk...'

'You aren't going to dictate terms to me, like Enrico Salvatore, are you?' he asked, his mouth twisting.

'I said we should talk! I don't want to dictate to you, any more than I want you to dictate to me! I think that was one thing that was wrong with our marriage—you still had some old-fashioned idea about being boss, and laying down the law in your own home and so on. I hate to tell you this, Sean, but Queen Victoria is dead, and we live in very different times. If our marriage is going to work it has to be on a strictly fifty-fifty basis. We discuss everything. We try to come to a mutually acceptable compromise.'

He nodded gravely. 'OK. Well, when we draw up our agenda for discussions, I'd like the first item to be a baby, Nadine. I know you are about to start off on an exciting new career, but I'm listening to the tick of time, and I want children, our children, yours and mine. From the minute my mother left me and my father, I never really had a family. Our lives fell apart after that, and I always promised myself that one day I'd belong to a family again, marry, have children. I was too busy to think of settling down for years, then I met you and we got married, but you wouldn't have a baby so I still haven't got my family!'

She looked at him with direct, darkened eyes. 'Is the baby a condition, Sean? If I won't have one yet, does that mean we don't get together again?'

He turned pale, his mouth tight, his gaze sombre. After a pause he sighed and shook his head. 'No, of course not. I want you, Nadine. Not your money. Not a baby. Just you. If you really don't want to have children I suppose I can learn to live with that, however hard it may be for me.' His mouth twisted. 'Maybe we should buy a dog? Would that give the house a family feel to it?'

She smiled tremulously. 'I love dogs. A cat would be just as nice; maybe both of them?' She put her arms around him and laid her head on his chest, listening to the beat of his heart under her ear. Sean held her, a hand on her hair, the other clenching on her waist possessively. 'But I do want babies,' she said. 'I always did mean to have them, sooner or later, it was just that I had other priorities at first, and I still do. But things will change now. I won't model any more, I'll concentrate on this chat show—so far I only have a contract for six shows, and if they don't pick my contract up again I'll be out of a job!'

'They'll pick it up,' Sean said drily. 'Greg tells me he's ready to bet on it that you'll be a success.'

'Did he?' Her eyes glowed. 'That's wonderful. I only hope he's right. But even if they do want another series of shows, there will be long gaps between each series. In the future I'll have far more free time. Give me a year, Sean, just one more year to see if I succeed in TV, then we'll try for a baby.'

He tightened his hold on her, laughing deep in his chest. 'That will be fun.'

She giggled. 'Well, we aren't starting just yet, so stop getting excited! And once the baby comes we'll work something out, get a part-time nanny, so that I can go on with my career and still be with the baby as often as possible.' She lifted her head, and looked up into his face, her eyes passionate. 'You must start trusting me, Sean. Give me space to make decisions of my own, and be prepared to talk over anything that's bothering you, instead of losing your temper and trying to browbeat me.'

He sighed heavily. 'The trouble is, when I'm worried or upset, it's hard to be calm and rational about it. My emotions run away with me, and I lose control.'

She looked at him with rueful tenderness. 'Yes,' she said, thinking that there was a lot of the little boy in him still, and maybe that was something else that could be laid at his mother's door. She had walked out at such a vital point in his adolescence, setting up a dangerous pattern in his emotional responses. Sean hadn't made the usual gradual transition from childhood to manhood; he had suddenly been left alone in a world he saw as treacherous. Oh, it explained so much! His creative impulses, his desire to bring order out of chaos, to arrange and interpret life on film—and his personality, his passion and insecurity, his explosive inner rage, his charm, his jealousy.

Nadine kissed him gently on the mouth and felt the immediate flare of passion between them, sensed his need surging upwards, his body quivering in hungry response.

'If we can only learn to trust each other, our marriage will work this time, darling,' she whispered, and Sean murmured back.

'Yes, darling.' But his mind was on other things; he was touching her with hands that were unsteady and breathing thickly. 'Nadine, let's get out of here,' he said hoarsely. 'Let's go home, I need to make love to you.'

'I need it, too,' she said, and hand in hand they walked out of the office and into their future.

INDULGE A LITTLE 6947 SWEEPSTAKES
NO PURCHASE NECESSARY

HERE'S HOW THE SWEEPSTAKES WORKS:
The Harlequin Reader Service shipments for January, February and March 1994 will contain, respectively, coupons for entry into three prize drawings: a trip for two to San Francisco, an Alaskan cruise for two and a trip for two to Hawaii. To be eligible for any drawing using an Entry Coupon, simply complete and mail according to directions.

There is no obligation to continue as a Reader Service subscriber to enter and be eligible for any prize drawing. You may also enter any drawing by hand printing your name and address on a 3" x 5" card and the destination of the prize you wish that entry to be considered for (i.e., San Francisco trip, Alaskan cruise or Hawaiian trip). Send your 3" x 5" entries to: Indulge a Little 6947 Sweepstakes, c/o Prize Destination you wish that entry to be considered for, P.O. Box 1315, Buffalo, NY 14269-1315, U.S.A. or Indulge a Little 6947 Sweepstakes, P.O. Box 610, Fort Erie, Ontario L2A 5X3, Canada.

To be eligible for the San Francisco trip, entries must be received by 4/30/94; for the Alaskan cruise, 5/31/94; and the Hawaiian trip, 6/30/94. No responsibility is assumed for lost, late or misdirected mail. Sweepstakes open to residents of the U.S. (except Puerto Rico) and Canada, 18 years of age or older. All applicable laws and regulations apply. Sweepstakes void wherever prohibited.

For a copy of the Official Rules, send a self-addressed, stamped envelope (WA residents need not affix return postage) to: Indulge a Little 6947 Rules, P.O. Box 4631, Blair, NE 68009, U.S.A.

INDR93

INDULGE A LITTLE 6947 SWEEPSTAKES
NO PURCHASE NECESSARY

HERE'S HOW THE SWEEPSTAKES WORKS:
The Harlequin Reader Service shipments for January, February and March 1994 will contain, respectively, coupons for entry into three prize drawings: a trip for two to San Francisco, an Alaskan cruise for two and a trip for two to Hawaii. To be eligible for any drawing using an Entry Coupon, simply complete and mail according to directions.

There is no obligation to continue as a Reader Service subscriber to enter and be eligible for any prize drawing. You may also enter any drawing by hand printing your name and address on a 3" x 5" card and the destination of the prize you wish that entry to be considered for (i.e., San Francisco trip, Alaskan cruise or Hawaiian trip). Send your 3" x 5" entries to: Indulge a Little 6947 Sweepstakes, c/o Prize Destination you wish that entry to be considered for, P.O. Box 1315, Buffalo, NY 14269-1315, U.S.A. or Indulge a Little 6947 Sweepstakes, P.O. Box 610, Fort Erie, Ontario L2A 5X3, Canada.

To be eligible for the San Francisco trip, entries must be received by 4/30/94; for the Alaskan cruise, 5/31/94; and the Hawaiian trip, 6/30/94. No responsibility is assumed for lost, late or misdirected mail. Sweepstakes open to residents of the U.S. (except Puerto Rico) and Canada, 18 years of age or older. All applicable laws and regulations apply. Sweepstakes void wherever prohibited.

For a copy of the Official Rules, send a self-addressed, stamped envelope (WA residents need not affix return postage) to: Indulge a Little 6947 Rules, P.O. Box 4631, Blair, NE 68009, U.S.A.

INDR93

INDULGE A LITTLE SWEEPSTAKES

OFFICIAL ENTRY COUPON

This entry must be received by: MAY 31, 1994
This month's winner will be notified by: JUNE 15, 1994
Trip must be taken between: JULY 31, 1994-JULY 31, 1995

YES, I want to win the Alaskan Cruise vacation for two. I understand that the prize includes round-trip airfare, one-week cruise including private cabin, all meals and pocket money as revealed on the "wallet" scratch-off card.

Name________________________________

Address ____________________ Apt. ____________

City________________________________

State/Prov.________________ Zip/Postal Code____________

Daytime phone number________________________
(Area Code)

Account #________________________________

Return entries with invoice in envelope provided. Each book in this shipment has two entry coupons—and the more coupons you enter, the better your chances of winning!

 MONTH2

INDULGE A LITTLE SWEEPSTAKES

OFFICIAL ENTRY COUPON

This entry must be received by: MAY 31, 1994
This month's winner will be notified by: JUNE 15, 1994
Trip must be taken between: JULY 31, 1994-JULY 31, 1995

YES, I want to win the Alaskan Cruise vacation for two. I understand that the prize includes round-trip airfare, one-week cruise including private cabin, all meals and pocket money as revealed on the "wallet" scratch-off card.

Name________________________________

Address ____________________ Apt. ____________

City________________________________

State/Prov.________________ Zip/Postal Code____________

Daytime phone number________________________
(Area Code)

Account #________________________________

Return entries with invoice in envelope provided. Each book in this shipment has two entry coupons—and the more coupons you enter, the better your chances of winning!

© 1993 HARLEQUIN ENTERPRISES LTD. MONTH2